Shadows Across the Sun

ALBERT LIKHANOV

Shadows Across the Sun

TRANSLATED FROM THE RUSSIAN BY
Richard Lourie

1 8  1 7

HARPER & ROW, PUBLISHERS

Cambridge, Philadelphia, San Francisco, London, Mexico City, São Paulo, Sydney

NEW YORK

"When In My Arms" translated by Babette Deutsch
from THE WORKS OF ALEXANDER PUSHKIN, by Alexander Pushkin,
edited by Avraham Yarmolinsky. Copyright 1936, renewed 1964 by
Random House, Inc. Reprinted by permission of the publisher.

SHADOWS ACROSS THE SUN
Copyright © 1977 by Albert Likhanov
Published by arrangement with VAAP, Moscow.
Originally published in *Yunost* magazine, Moscow, 1977.
First hardcover publication by Moldaya Gvardia, Moscow, 1979.
Translation copyright © 1983 by Harper & Row, Publishers, Inc.
First American Edition
10 9 8 7 6 5 4 3 2 1

Library of Congress Cataloging in Publication Data
Likhanov, Al'bert Anatol'evich.
   Shadows across the sun.

   Translation of: Solnechnoe zatmenie.
   Summary: A disabled girl and a lonely boy discover
first love in their small neighborhood in Moscow.
   [1. Soviet Union—Fiction.   2. Physically handicapped
—Fiction]   I. Title.
PZ7.L6268Sh 1983   891.73'44 [Fic]   80-8440
ISBN 0-06-023868-2
ISBN 0-06-023869-0 (lib. bdg.)

Shadows Across the Sun

I

It wasn't a typical city outskirts, bristling with tall concrete apartment houses. From a distance they look like some fairy-tale city shimmering with a thousand eyes and holding out the promise of enchantment—until you come closer, then they turn into barriers of stone. You turn one block after another hoping to come upon some open space, some patch of earth, a field of dandelions. But instead of dandelions there's just another block of apartments, then another, and yet another. Your energy begins to flag, you can't find your way out, and the gray asphalt wearies your eyes.

This enclave was tucked away in between the city's center and the new districts. It still had old wooden houses, rickety barracks dating back to the war, and there was earth to be seen, and dandelions, and in the springtime the old bird-cherry trees dropped their petals on the wooden sidewalks.

There was such peace and contentment there that you forgot it was part of a large, noisy city. And people getting off the trolleybus that ran past the acacias, with briefcases or shopping bags, would automatically begin to slow down as they rounded the trees and entered that old enclave where they'd been living for so many years. They would look around, their eyes refreshed and curious again, and they would feel relaxed. This little nook, sheltered from all the hustle and bustle by its poplars, shrubbery, and benign quiet, lived at a different rhythm, breathed at a different rate, and everyone who entered it surrendered to its influence.

Fedya's father was the only one who did not slow his step. He forged ahead, rounded the acacias, and pressed on, kicking up little clouds of dust. Fedya watched him from his pigeon cote, as if by accompanying his father with his eyes he could keep him out of trouble.

His father's path led to an open stall made of plywood, with a roof of yellow corrugated plastic, the most modern structure in the district. This was a beer stall, and there was always a bunch of men around it, a whirlpool that only stopped swirling when night fell. For Fedya it was the saddest of places, not only in the town but in his life.

There were plenty of other frustrations and set-backs in life, of course—bad marks at school, fights with other pigeon fanciers; that was normal, no get-ting around that—and there were times when his father beat him. But compared with that damned beer stall, all the rest was nothing, a cut you spit on and rubbed away. Because nothing hurts more than seeing one's own father disgraced.

Fedya's father was charging straight home, plow-ing up the dust with his battered boots that were white at the toes. He didn't see the bird-cherry trees, the grass, the clouds. He was too absorbed, his eyes on the ground as if he were sunk in serious thought. Fedya stared at him. Often his penetrating look seemed to help—his father would walk right past the beer stall. But if Fedya even blinked or glanced at a pigeon or let his mind wander, then it would all start.

"Hey!" someone would shout in a hoarse voice from the beer stall. "John Ivanovich, steer for port!" Or, even worse, "Hey, you American, get your ass over here!" Then they'd all laugh.

His father would swing around and head for the

beer stall, shouting belligerently, "Who's calling me names? Who?" But they'd fling their arms around him and slur drunkenly, "Cut it out, Gera, let's have a round." And he would hang around the beer stall until late. And when he did come home, the room where Fedya lived with his parents would fill with the stink of beer.

His mother didn't cry anymore. She looked at his father with eyes that had gone dry; she had dried up too, like a board. She was lean and sallow, an old woman now. His father would wheeze, take off his boots, and say in defense of himself, "What's the matter, Tonya? I'm not drunk. I just had one little mug, that's all."

It wasn't the mug that mattered—he could have three, or five if he wanted. That wasn't what broke Fedya's heart—it was the shame of it all. His father's shame. His unmanly weakness.

Fedya's father's name really was John Ivanovich. He had been born in the thirties, well before the war. At that time there had been a fashion in unusual names. Nowadays there are fashions in boots, those high boots that fit like stockings, (there was always a terrible line for them at the shoe store near where they lived). In those days there had been a fashion in names. So his parents gave him an

American name—John. He could have changed his name, and he did change it whenever he met new people. He'd tell them his name was Georgi, but the people around here knew his real name and they laughed at him. Fedya's mother said they did it because his father had lived in the same building in the same part of town since he was a kid, and all those poor drunks had been his childhood friends.

Fedya thought about them a lot. There was one who looked all gray and used a cane and had been his father's friend since they were both kids. And then there was the redhead, and the bald one with the potbelly. They blew the foam off their mugs and clinked them with his father. Fedya looked at them from his pigeon cote and could not imagine them as boys. Had they ever really been boys? It seemed too weird. And stupid too. Even if they all were buddies and had lived there for a hundred years—why should they call his father names? Why did they go on needling him when they were old and gray? What had his father ever done to them? That one with the gray hair, and Platonov, they never called him by his first name, always just Platonov, and the bald one's name was Yegor. But his father had to be the American. The American. John. A grown man and they still called him the American.

Anybody else would have told those old buddies to go to hell. He should walk past that beer stall. Not let them get to him. But his father seemed to have some hidden weak spot, some lack of courage he could never overcome. Here he was coming around the corner, heading for home, absorbed in his thoughts, his head down. Now he was even with the beer stall.

"Uncle Sam!" shouted the bald one. "Hello! Steer for port, I got an advance on my pay!"

His father stood still for a moment, then shrugged his shoulders and went over to the stall, shouting in a heartbreaking voice, "Who called me Uncle Sam?" The men laughed, holding their bellies. If it were only his three old friends . . . but they were all making fun of him.

A clown.

Watching his father turn off toward the stall, Fedya bit his lip and drove his axe angrily into the wood. Aw, the hell with him! The grave's the only cure for a hunchback. That was his mother's saying, but he often used it too.

Fedya didn't have any friends for a very simple reason: He didn't want to be called an American like his father. Though he would never have let that happen—anyone who tried that would get a good smack in the teeth. Just let them try and call him that! But all the same, he didn't hang around much with other boys because he was ashamed of his father. Plenty of fathers drank—that was nothing. But nobody's father was jeered at like his. So Fedya spent most of his time alone.

Fedya was used to being alone with his pigeons. With some old boards, swiped from a construction site, and an old piece of wire netting, he was making his new pigeon cote. He worked quietly, singing to himself a funny little song, one he'd heard at the movies or on the radio, he couldn't remember where.

> "I don't need a Turkish shore,
> I don't need an Africa . . ."

That was all he could remember, but still it suited his mood. After all, what did he want with Turkish shores or with Africa? He was fine just where he was. In his own little spot. It was summer. The tumbler pigeons cooed, their crops swelled. A golden male spread his tail in front of a female, wanting to show off for her. Those flying devils! Just wait till your Fedya finishes your new cote, a pigeon cote to end all pigeon cotes, with plenty of room. And it won't just sit on the roof, but it will have four strong legs and a sloping top, built just right, so the rain won't drip in.

He thought of his father again and his fingers slackened, the hammer fell from his hand. His fingers felt cold. It was always like that—he could be thinking about all sorts of different things, but as soon as he thought about his father, his palms would start to sweat and his mood would be spoiled.

Fedya turned toward the beer stall. His father was making his way home now, in no hurry anymore. He was holding his head up proud and high, twisting it around on his thin neck as if trying to attract attention. Fedya shook his head and went back to work. A good, clean smell arose from the wood shavings and seemed to clear his head. Fedya looked at his tumblers and the deep-blue sky overhead with a more cheerful eye now. Did the sky have an end? he wondered. He nailed the netting to the frame. People said that pilots loved the sky more than anyone else, but he didn't agree. It wasn't pilots, it was pigeon fanciers who really loved the sky. A pilot could fly whenever he wanted. But a person who stood on the ground or on a roof and whistled to his pigeons felt all the joy of their soaring flight. And there were times when he felt as if it weren't the pigeons, but he himself who was up there, flying through the blue sky, his wings quivering and flapping. He never told anyone about that feeling. He wasn't much of a talker, and besides, how could you explain that to anyone? He would lean against a post, tilt back his head, and fly off into the sky's depths until he felt a pang of fear in the pit of his stomach. . . .

2

Lena had been watching Fedya for a week now, ever since they brought her home. She knew his name. The pigeon cote he was building was almost level with her third-floor window, and she could hear every word, every whisper, spoken there.

But Fedya didn't have the faintest idea she even existed.

The wind fluttered the curtain, bringing Lena the scent of fresh wood shavings, a smell she had never experienced before. She shivered with a desire to bury her face in a pile of those shavings and breathe in their enticing aroma until her head spun from dizziness. All she had to do was ask her mother or father, and they would bring her all the shavings she wanted. But Lena said nothing to them, as if to savor the postponed pleasure.

In the mornings when she woke up, she would listen to the sounds coming from outside—the pigeons murmuring in their cote, the ding of the trolley bells as they swung around, their iron wheels grinding on the tracks. Out past the acacias the trolleys' crossbars were always tearing loose and jangling against the wires.

But when Fedya appeared, everything else vanished for Lena. There was only the rasp of his plane on the wood, the strokes of his axe, and his husky voice occasionally singing:

"I don't need a Turkish shore,
I don't need an Africa . . ."

Lena would roll her wheelchair over to the window and move the curtain aside to watch him. But as soon as Fedya lifted his head, she would wheel herself away in fright. She didn't want him to see her. She wanted to remain invisible. That was the fun of it. But maybe fun wasn't the right word. Maybe it was something else.

Lena had been feeling strange. This was her own home, but she wasn't used to it and did not feel at home here. As far back as she could remember, home had been the boarding school, the grounds around it, the room she shared with nine other girls like herself and their nurse, Dusya. Before that she had been in a nursery school, in a forest outside the city. She felt at home in all the noise and hubbub of the boarding school. Sometimes it was quiet, but it was a special kind of quiet, not like the quiet at home, where she was all alone and shut off from the world. In the quiet moments at the boarding school, the girls would cry at some sad story; they liked sad things—they knew what they meant. Late in the evenings, when the teachers had all gone home and Nurse Dusya dozed in her little cubicle, they would all cry softly together, which in some strange way brought them even closer together.

There was no time for sadness in the morning—in the morning they had to get dressed, doing the best they could; pulling themselves into their wheelchairs, hobbling around and helping each other pull on their dresses; laughing, shouting, crying too. But in the daytime their crying had something oddly cheerful about it. To cry sadly in the daytime was against the rules. Their own rules.

But everything was different at home. The days passed, lonely and empty. Things would become lively in the evening when her mother and father came home from work.

During the day nothing interested her besides

Fedya. He sang, he mumbled to himself, he talked to his pigeons, and he planed his boards. And he never guessed he was being watched through a gap in the curtains by a girl who could move about only in a wheelchair.

That wheelchair! When she was in boarding school in a room with nine other girls like herself, her wheelchair seemed somehow alive to her, she could even talk to it.

They had all had the same illness—polio—and that seemed to bring them closer together and give them a common identity. The room with its ten beds was not just a dormitory for girls with a crippling illness but something else entirely. Zina, Lena's friend who was one of the most serious cases—one of her arms and one of her legs were paralyzed—once said that their room was a skeet. When she said that, everyone had stopped talking. A skeet was a small monastery set deep in the Siberian taiga where monks secluded themselves from life. Lena didn't agree.

Their room was no skeet! The walls were covered with embroideries, pictures of their favorite actors, bright orange sweetbriar berries strung into necklaces, pretty New Year's cards from home, and a portrait of Lenin that they had bought the previous year when they had joined the Young Communist League.

Everyone fitted in. There they were just people—equal, open, and straightforward, cheerful more often than not, with no low spirits allowed—they were merciless when it came to fighting despondency and other such moods. Vera Ilyinichna had come to teach them when they were in the sixth grade. At first she had been unable to control her emotions. Every once in a while when she looked at them, her eyes would fill with tears—for no reason at all. The girls were a constant amazement to her. Once, during a literature class, the girls wanted to discuss *The Young Guard*, a book they'd been waiting to read since the fifth grade. Now they discussed it with such enthusiasm that Vera Ilyinichna was stunned into silence. At the end of the lesson she told them that in her other school, the regular one, her eighth-grade pupils didn't pay attention and would get all the characters mixed up. Vera Ilyinichna explained that those students were too flighty and had no time for books—all they thought about was dancing or strolling down Broadway, as they called one of the streets in their town.

The girls did not say a word when their teacher had finished talking. Finally Lena broke the silence:

"Vera Ilyinichna, we're glad to have you as our class mother, you're a good person. But you have one fault. You musn't feel sorry for us."

When the girls left the classroom, Vera Ilyinichna remained behind with Lena. She helped Lena from her desk to her wheelchair and wheeled her to the dormitory. Lena felt something was bothering her teacher.

"Why did you say that to me?" she finally asked Lena.

"That's what what we tell all new teachers. Besides," Lena added, "we've chosen you as our class mother."

"Thank you," said Vera Ilyinichna, her voice constrained.

"Stop a minute, please," ordered Lena, "and bend down."

Vera Ilyinichna bent forward and Lena put her arms around her teacher's neck, and kissed her. Vera Ilyinichna quickly disappeared behind Lena— it was too much for her. Lena could hear her nose making a sniffling sound.

"There you go again." Lena sighed reproachfully. "I didn't kiss you so you'd give me good marks, so don't think that. I'll get them anyway. It's because I like you."

From then on no tears came to Vera Ilyinichna's eyes, at least not in front of her class, and she never again mentioned her other eighth-grade students.

Yes, they had an unusual life at the boarding school—wheelchairs and crutches, paralyzed arms and legs, beauty and ugliness, meant absolutely nothing there. It was a life with a different scale of values, where warmth and love and feeling were what mattered. But here at home . . .

When Lena found herself alone in her own home, everything started to change. She looked out the window. Normal people were walking down the street. Little girls were skipping rope. And there was a pigeon cote and a funny boy with green eyes who planed boards, hammered nails, and all of a sudden would start to sing:

> "I don't need a Turkish shore,
> I don't need an Africa . . ."

That made Lena laugh, but not the way she laughed at boarding school; there she would have laughed out loud, but here she clapped her hand to her mouth so that he wouldn't hear. Wouldn't hear her laughing and see her in that ugly, horrible, shameful wheelchair!

3

Fedya reveled in his pigeons' flight. He waited until they had flown back into the cote, then he counted them, closed the netting, and started planing again when he heard his mother's voice.

"Fedya! Fedya!"

He looked down, and the sight of her wrenched his heart. Her narrow shoulders drooped, her features had grown sharper, and because she was looking up at him she seemed to be pleading for him to run down and help her.

He climbed down and she handed him two sausage sandwiches wrapped in newspaper. No explanations were necessary. She had not called him home for supper because things were too unbearable there.

"How nice those shavings smell," she said. "I'll sit here awhile."

She sat down on the ladder that led up to the cote and said, "I wish I were a boy. I'd fly pigeons with you."

That was all she said. Fedya chewed his sausage, aware of her silence. He felt like crying. God! What did these grown-ups think they were doing, anyway! Even he had brains enough to see that was no way to live. There was the sky, all blue, and the poplars rustling their leaves, and the pigeons cooing and people walking by—everything around was so clear and bright and good. With that all around, why couldn't they make life clear and bright and good, too? Be good to one another, rejoice together, love each other, be happy—why not? Fedya felt so unhappy that he lost his desire to eat. He felt sorry for his mother, not himself. Just look at her—she wasn't herself anymore. There was a picture of her on the wall at home, a beautiful woman with dark, dark eyes and a braid thick as your wrist. And though the picture was old and faded, you could still see that she had been happy and cheerful, and everything had been fine then.

Fedya forced down the last of his sausage.

"You know what?" he said for the sake of saying

something. "I got an offer to sell some of my tumblers. There's a man over on the next block, people say he's a retired colonel. And filthy rich too. He came over and he's interested."

His mother sighed.

"It's a sin to sell birds—they're living creatures. And free!"

She sighed again and turned away. He knew there were tears in her eyes.

"There you go again," said Fedya.

She shook her head and turned back to him. Her wrinkles went from her eyes to her temples and from her nose to the corners of her mouth. But she wasn't crying. Her eyes were dry and had a sharp look to them.

"Sit down next to me. We've got to talk," she said.

He sat down obediently among the shavings on the grass.

"It's no good talking to your father," she said with an apologetic smile. "So I want to talk things over with you. Don't worry, I won't cry."

Fedya nodded, looking at her gray, unhealthy face.

"I need your help, son. If not that, at least your approval. . . . I can't go on any longer. My strength is gone. My life is no life, it's a prison. I know it's not easy for you either, but my back's to the wall now. I can't go on like this any longer."

She fell silent, looking at him, then she lowered her eyes.

"Let's go away, Fedya," she pleaded, still looking off to one side. "There's plenty of other towns in the world. We can go to your grandmother's."

Now Fedya took his eyes off his mother and stared intensely at his pigeon cote.

"Would you be sorry to leave them?"

Fedya shook his head.

"Father." He nearly made a slip of the tongue and said, "The American."

Before she could answer, Fedya's father appeared as if by magic. He walked briskly over to them, sat down next to Fedya on the shavings, and put an arm around him. Fedya shook it off.

"So that's how it is!" his father cried. "You open up your heart and they turn up their noses! Where will you go?"

Fedya's mother was still looking away as if she had not noticed him.

"For God's sake tell me what's going on. What have I ever done to you? Am I some kind of drunken bum? I never spent a night at the police station. Just take a look at some of them, sprawled in the gutter.

That's not me. I like my beer, sure, what's wrong with that? And so what if I like to talk with my old buddies, is that a crime?"

Fedya's mother was still keeping her silence while he looked right at his father. His mother wanted them to leave his father. To go to Grandma's. To another town. He couldn't do that! His father wasn't a drunken bum, a barroom brawler. No, he was just pitiful. Thin, with black stubble growing over his sunken cheeks. And he always seemed to be begging. From everybody. Just as he was doing right now.

Fedya looked at his mother. She was like an impregnable fortress. All his father's words bounced off her. His father always made many promises, and all of them empty.

"You know what, Dad," began Fedya, but then broke off. His father too was silent, as though waiting for some words, any sort of words, angry or kind, and he seemed to be begging for those words from his wife, like alms. "You know, Dad, of course, you're no drunken bum. You're just—just a nothing, that's all."

His father turned his head as if he'd been struck in the face. He closed his eyes and sighed. "A nothing? What do you mean? What are you saying?"

But Fedya did not reply. Out of the corner of his eye he saw his mother looking at him with curiosity. He had just told her he was sorry for his father, for the American, and now he had as good as slapped his face. A nothing! He had said he was a nothing.

For a moment his father didn't move, then he staggered over to a tree and leaned against it. Suddenly Fedya saw his father's shoulders shaking. He was crying. Sobbing. People stopped and looked at him. Platonov shouted down from his balcony: "Gera, Gera! What's wrong?"

Fedya couldn't stand it anymore. Pity for his father rolled onto his heart like a great stone and he too burst into tears. He bawled like a baby, inconsolably, at the top of his lungs. And through his tears he wailed at his mother: "What are you doing, what are you grown-ups doing?"

His mother burst into tears too. Shaking her tears away, she raced past Fedya to his father, took him by the shoulders, and led him home, shamed before all the world.

Fedya watched them through his tears. His father and mother seemed pitiful, downtrodden, insulted. In despair he asked himself, Why? Why? It was crazy—here were two grown-up people who loved each other, they really did, and yet they kept on tormenting each other. Why? For what? Just because of that beer stall and the stupid name, John Ivanovich? Such petty little things! How could that keep them from having a happy, peaceful life, all three of them? Why couldn't they stand by each other, give each other strength, and live like human beings?

Fedya picked up his axe, hammer, and plane, climbed the ladder, and tossed his things into the cote. Then he bolted the cote shut and climbed back down. His foot slipped and he fell onto his side. As he slid down, he caught a glimpse of the corner of the pigeon cote, the pale clear sky, and part of a window with a frightened face. He jumped up and ran limping off home, home to the old two-story barracks built during the war. To the dark doorway through which his parents had just vanished.

4

Lena was that sort of person—she couldn't just sit quietly and watch people quarrel. Back in boarding school she had her own way of ending quarrels. Whenever she saw a bunch of girls shouting and making angry gestures, she would get her wheelchair going at top speed and zoom straight at them, shouting, "Out of my way!"

A few times her wheels actually did run into someone and cause them some pain, but people realized why she was barreling down on them, and once an argument was broken up, it would feel pointless to start it up all over again.

She had been sitting well back in the room, suffering through the whole scene in silence, but when she heard Fedya crying she couldn't bear it any-

more. She went to the window and pulled the curtains aside, ready to shout something—but she was too late, the grown-ups were gone. Then she saw Fedya clamber down the ladder, fall, hop back to his feet, and run off to the old barracks where he lived.

Lena closed the curtains and circled the room a couple of times, trying to calm down but with little success.

Oh God, she thought, everyone has some problem, some pain. Isn't there one house, one family in the entire world where everything's all right? Where people are peaceful and happy?

She glanced up at the wall, at the photograph of her mother, her father, and herself taken one Sunday afternoon on the school grounds by an obnoxious man with a smooth, ingratiating, foxy little face. He had appeared unexpectedly in front of the parents and their crippled children, offering to photograph them so they could have a keepsake. A keepsake of what? The parents were thrown into confusion. Lena saw how upset her own parents looked. The man with the foxy face positioned her parents symmetrically on either side of her wheelchair, then ran nimbly back to his camera and clicked the shutter several times. And now that "keepsake" was hanging on the wall at home, next to a picture of Lena in the boarding-school dormitory.

She smiled grimly as she remembered the photographer. "A keepsake, huh." Lena laughed, but she didn't feel amused. She looked more closely at the picture. There was her mother, round faced, fair-haired, and blue eyed. She didn't have a single line or wrinkle on her face, and anyone who didn't know her would think she didn't have a care in the world. But her mother's eyes always betrayed her—she would have sudden attacks of blinking. She blinked when she was unhappy and when things weren't going well. On visitors' Sundays she would always start blinking as soon as she saw Lena. Then she would start hugging and kissing her, as if they were saying good-bye forever.

Lena hated that. She would start feeling angry as soon as she saw her mother. She wished her mother could have been a little tougher—things would have been much easier for Lena then. Lena always said what was on her mind without mincing any words, but it didn't seem to have any effect on her mother. Maybe it was because she was too busy blinking to notice what was going on around her.

Her father, that was a different story. He was a real person. Not that Lena thought her mother wasn't a real person, but her father had the sort of character that demanded respect. Pyotr Silich. Even his name sounded impressive. Lena was tremendously proud of her father. He was a talented geologist who had discovered nickel deposits in Siberia. He was always off to Siberia, from where he would send Lena envelopes stuffed with photographs, postcards, and badges. He always wrote on the back of the photographs in his neat handwriting: "Urengoi. There is going to be a major railroad station here." "Udoken. Huge copper deposits. My colleagues are still prospecting in this area." "Look, my daughter, what a river. It was named after you. It's called the Lena."

Lena squealed with joy whenever she received one of those fat envelopes from her father, and would read all the captions aloud to the other girls. Then they would crowd around the large world atlas and find Urengoi and Udoken, and sail down the Lena River in their imaginations.

Her father was sensitive to other people's feelings. In his letters he never raved about or described the beauty and wonders of Siberia, he simply explained what was in the photographs. Once when Lena persuaded him to come to their school to give a talk, he spoke of his profession very prosaically and made it sound dry.

Lena listened to his talk with great satisfaction, glad to have such a wise, tactful father. After the talk Lena was allowed to go out onto the grounds with him. It was late autumn, October, and there was a fine drizzle in the air. The air smelled of fallen leaves. Her father coughed and muttered behind her, "I just can't understand why you insisted I give a talk here."

"Because I wanted everyone to know what my father is like," said Lena. "And besides," she added, "we can't cut ourselves off from life altogether."

Her father coughed again and Lena smiled. She felt uncomfortable when people talked to her from behind. But this time it was all right. She loved her father, and even though she couldn't see his face, she could hear his deep cough.

"A keepsake." Did they really think of it like that, as something to remember her by? Had it always been like that? The fact that she was still alive and had made it to eighth grade must have seemed wrong, unnatural. She'd be gone soon. And they were afraid. Afraid to repeat those casual words—"a keepsake." A keepsake of what? Of her, of course!

Lena wheeled herself away from the photograph. It all comes from being alone all day long, she thought. Alone in a room with no one around. In the boarding school she would never have let herself slide like that and think about such nonsense. It's egotism too, she decided. I'm only thinking about myself. Take that boy, Fedya. Are things any easier for him even though his arms and legs are normal? She went to the window and again asked herself: Can it be that no one in the world is truly happy, completely happy? Aren't there any happy people at all? She shook her head. What a stupid idea! Of course there are happy people! There are! There are!

A key turned in the door and her mother appeared in the doorway, pretty and laughing, her father smiling at Lena from behind her. Lena wheeled herself over to them as fast as she could.

"Lena, I've got great news!" cried her mother. "I'm quitting my job."

Lena brought her chair to a halt.

"But why? Why?" she cried desperately.

"Let's not have any discussion about it," said her mother.

Lena felt as if she were turning to stone inside. So they noticed it, she thought. They just didn't say anything. They noticed I've changed. That I've been letting myself think all sorts of stupid things.

"Mother," she said, her voice steely, emphasizing

each word, "you needn't do it for my sake."

A wry smile, barely visible, played over Lena's lips.

"If you leave your job," she said, "I'll know you think of me as a useless, helpless invalid who can't take care of herself."

"Have you lost your mind?" exclaimed Lena's mother, blinking furiously.

"It's either or. Either you keep on working or you can take me home."

"Where?"

"To boarding school," Lena corrected herself.

"But, Lena, you were ill, you had pleural pneumonia," Lena's father said after a preliminary cough.

"And what else?" asked Lena. "What else is on your list?"

"Nothing," he said.

"Comrades, parents," said Lena didactically, repelled by her own tone of voice. "Let's drop the subject once and for all. I will not be treated like a helpless invalid."

Her mother blinked, ready to burst into tears. Her father sighed.

"All right, Lena," he mumbled, "the subject is closed."

Lena watched them go into the kitchen, unpack

the groceries, opening and closing the refrigerator door, without saying a word. Then they both sighed loudly at the same time. Lena burst out laughing.

"What are you laughing about?" asked her father.

"I'm just glad we settled that," said Lena. If only everyone's problems could be solved as easily as they had just solved theirs, thought Lena, her mind on Fedya and his problems.

That evening as they were having tea, Lena said to her mother, "Mother, I have a funny favor to ask of you."

Her mother blinked rapidly, afraid of what was coming next.

"Buy me a long beautiful dress!"

5

Fedya hurried out to his pigeons. It had taken him a long time to fall asleep the night before. And then he had had a nightmare in which the dough his mother set out began to rise and rise, overflowing the bowl. It spread across the floor, swelling and rising until it rose up to his chin and began to choke him. There was nothing he could do to free himself. It was too thick to swim through and too slippery to walk on.

When he woke up he felt deserted and uncomfortable. His parents had gone off to work. Their empty bed was rumpled, there were shoes scattered on the floor. The bread on the table was crumbled and cut, and the dishes hadn't been washed. Only the sun lent the room a touch of warmth as it cast bright patches on the dirty floor and messy table. It seemed to be trying to tell him something. He jumped out of bed. It was simple! The table was dirty but he could clean it if he wanted to. Where was the rag? There it was. One, two, three, and it was done. The freshly cleaned oilcloth gleamed, but Fedya didn't stop to admire it—he was already carrying in a bucket of water. Just a little work and the floor would shine like new. Yes, that was more like it. All you had to do was really want something, and make up your mind to do it.

The room was becoming cleaner and nicer by the minute. Fedya made the beds, washed the dishes, put a clean tablecloth and a vase on the table, then ran out to break off a few hollyhocks. He wiped off the record player, took out a few records, and put "The Waves of the Amur" on for his father. His father had served in the Navy in the Far East. The Amur River was in that part of the world, and so he'd like hearing that song. Fedya looked around, pleased with his work. He filled his pockets with millet and crumbs for the pigeons and set off for his cote. He was way behind schedule.

The pigeons grumbled at him. They were angry and grumbling because he was late. He tossed them some millet, crumbled up the bread, and gave them fresh water; now they could fly out and enjoy themselves. He slid back the bolt and opened up the sky to the birds. They stirred and fluttered, then streaked up into the heights and began making circles. Fedya whistled after them, a long, trilling, quavering whistle, and watched them flying around and around in spirals until his neck started to ache. When he lowered his head, he noticed a movement in the curtain of the window across from his pigeon cote.

Then he remembered. Yesterday, after the talk and the tears, when he was running after his parents and fell, he had caught sight of a girl in that window.

His first feeling was one of annoyance. She must have heard everything.

But he had never seen any girl in that window before; only two people lived there, a man and his wife. He was a geologist, Pyotr Silich. Fedya knew his name because he had come over to the cote a few times and asked which were the tumblers and what made them different from the other pigeons. But who was that girl?

Fedya whistled softly. The curtains did not stir. He tried to remember her face, but he couldn't. No, there couldn't have been anyone there.

"Hello," he said softly. "Hey, girl!"

Nothing stirred behind the curtain. Maybe it was the wind. He picked up his plane and started to work on a board, glancing up at the window every now and again. No, nobody there. But something kept drawing his eyes to the window. He put down his plane. A funny idea came to his head.

"I know you're there looking at me," he said. No response. "What's the point of peeking through the curtains? You don't have to." No answer. He tucked his shirt neatly into his pants. "All right, then I'll climb up the drainpipe and see if you're there or not."

Fedya stamped his boots, climbed down the ladder, and looked up at the window again.

The curtains parted and Fedya saw a girl looking down at him. His heart stopped for a moment—she was so beautiful. Her delicate white face was surrounded by the golden color of wheat and the sun, a thick braid wound around her head and draped down one of her shoulders.

"So there," he said awkwardly.

"What did you say?" she asked.

"That you were there."

"All right, I'm here. So what?"

Somewhat embarrassed, Fedya shrugged his shoulders. "I don't know. Just that you're there."

Fedya could see that she felt awkward because he had made her look out the window; her pale face was slowly breaking out in a blush.

"Why were you watching me?"

"No special reason," she said flatly. "Just looking. Is there a law against it?"

Suddenly it all seemed very funny. He laughed. But his laugh confused her. Fedya saw her make a quick movement, as if she were going to close the curtains but then changed her mind.

"Why don't you come out? I'll show you my pigeons and you can pet them if you like."

He threw his head back and gave a long, piercing, masterly whistle, showing off a little for her.

"They're fine pigeons, Fedya," said the girl.

That made him wilt. It meant that she had heard everything. For a moment neither of them said anything.

"Well, what of it?" Fedya heard himself saying. "We've all got our problems. And there's nothing funny about it. It's all pretty sad. But from now on"—he sliced the air decisively with his hand—"it's all going to change."

He looked at the girl and his heart beat quicker again. "What's your name?"

"Lena."

"Well, you'll see, Lena," said Fedya, feeling his Adam's apple bob. "Today, at six o'clock, the three of us will come down that path, right past your window." He lowered his head and frowned. He could picture her sitting behind the curtain yesterday, listening to everything his mother and father had said. And she had heard him crying, too!

He felt so embarrassed, he did not look at her again. He climbed up to his cote, waited until the birds had flown in, closed everything up, and clambered down. Only then did he look up at Lena again. She was sitting just as she had been before, in a leather armchair, looking down at him with some expression like embarrassment on her face. Fedya nodded to her in gratitude and smiled. Then he said apologetically, "I wish you hadn't heard all that."

She didn't answer immediately, and when she did, it seemed to cost her some effort. "It doesn't matter. I've heard worse."

Fedya sighed and turned to go. He took a few steps, then ran back and shouted, "So you'll come see my pigeon cote?"

Lena did not answer.

"Will you come?" he asked one more time. She nodded, and Fedya's heart leaped. He had never seen a girl like her, a girl that beautiful.

All day Fedya rushed around feverishly. He went to one store for sausage and eggs, to others for milk and bread. It felt as if he were in a dream. Lena's face was always before his eyes.

A wheat-colored braid wound around her head and huge, dark-blue eyes—like the face on an ikon.

Who was she? he wondered. Where had she come from? Just out of nowhere? He could have kicked himself for being so dense—he'd been talking to her, he could have asked, hard as that might have been. But no, he really couldn't. He couldn't just start asking about every last little thing. She wasn't just any girl. She was special.

Fedya found strange, silly, unfamiliar words popping into his head. Words that had never entered his mind before. Beautiful—he had always reserved that word for pigeons or a picture of one of Raphael's paintings in a magazine. But for a person? And a girl?

Everything was swirling around in him. Some wall had crumbled down and something new emerged inside him. He didn't know if it was good or bad, but he did know there was some change going on.

He kept thinking about Lena. Lena and nothing else but.

Fedya even bumped into an old woman in a store, and when she called him a blind oaf he only replied with a foolish grin. And she of course thought that he was making fun of her.

It really was a magical day. Fedya remembered what had happened that morning—all you needed was to really want something!

At four o'clock he was finally ready. He took a bus to the construction site where his father worked.

The shovel on his father's steam shovel rumbled as it dumped a load of earth into a waiting truck. Fedya had to stop and admire it. The power of that machine! What a load it picked up in one bite! And his father ran it easily, as if playing with a toy. That weakling, that "nothing," as Fedya had called him yesterday. Fedya was determined to change all that. John Ivanovich was okay, nothing wrong in that. But not "the American," not Uncle Sam. Not a buffoon.

He sat to wait for the end of the shift. At last he spotted his father walking along, wiping his hands on some rags. He didn't look like a clown or a drunk, he looked like a plain, ordinary man.

When he saw Fedya, he seemed to stumble a little. "Is this your own idea?" he muttered gloomily.

"You think it was Ma's?"

As they walked together to the bus stop, his father

kept shaking his head and mumbling to himself.

"It was a good idea, Fedya," he finally said when they got onto the trolleybus.

They got off at their stop, walking slowly like everyone else. The stone city receded and they entered their little enclave of acacias, grass, and a few belated dandelions.

The beer stall was busy. The gray-haired man and Platonov were already there. Fedya tensed, ready to charge that stall and tear it down, beer, old buddies, and all. His father had a sense of what his son was feeling and said, "Fedya, give me your hand." And he took hold of Fedya's clenched fist.

It would have been hard to say who was leading whom as they walked calmly past the beer stall and down the dusty, trampled path past the pigeon cote.

"How are your tumblers?" asked his father, but the words seemed muffled and distant to Fedya. Fedya wasn't looking at his pigeon cote but at Lena's window.

She was there, waiting for him. He nodded to her, almost bursting with excitement. And then he realized that since their morning talk, he had been avoiding that path even though it was a shortcut.

6

As Fedya and his father vanished in their entrance-way, Lena drew the curtains and moved away from the window.

It had been a crazy day. A funny day. A strange day.

She wheeled herself around the room, spinning in circles and laughing as she remembered that crazy day. She would giggle foolishly or burst out laughing like an idiot. So that was Fedya! With his Turkish shore or an Africa. He needed them all right! He had pulled her out of herself like a snail from its shell. *Snail, snail, peep out of your shell, Snail, snail, I'll give you some pie. Snail, snail, now promise to tell, Will there be sun or clouds in the sky?* She repeated the old nursery rhyme to herself. That's what Fedya had said to her, not in those words, but that's what he had said. And the silly little snail had gotten all mixed up and peeped her head out.

She had kept herself well hidden for almost a month. She had listened to him humming, hammering, planing his boards. And now she had gotten caught at it. A boy who'd get what he wanted, no doubt about that.

Lena turned over in her mind the few things he had said, the simple words he had used; she turned them over like ornaments, precious things, and laughed again. "Hello," he had said. "Hey, girl!" Hey indeed! But then later on he had also said, "I wish you hadn't heard all that." And the way he had explained what was going to happen, and that determined gesture of his. Did that mean that Fedya was going to be leading his father home from work every day like a child, by the hand?

Lena paused for a moment. It was hard for her to understand. Her parents were always circling around her, like planets around a star. And her class mother, Vera Ilyinichna, had been selflessly devoted to her pupils. And Nurse Dusya surrounded them with loving sympathy day and night, speaking to them with old-fashioned words of tenderness, compassion. . . . It was time somebody had a little compassion for Fedya.

Lena had often seen Fedya's father standing at the beer stall. There were always plenty of men swirling around that stall, like a whirlpool. But before it had meant nothing to her, it had been alien to her. Now that alien thing had reached out and touched her.

"But what is the point of it all?" she asked herself aloud, and circled around the room again.

"I'm the point," she answered herself, glancing in the mirror. She laughed. "Me, me!" Then she wheeled herself close to the mirror.

At boarding school they had forbidden themselves to spend too much time in front of mirrors. The absolute minimum. To comb your hair and make sure you looked all right—and that was all. To stare at yourself was apt to set you thinking, and not the best kind of thoughts either. Zina used to say grimly, "There's no sense in it for us. We aren't women and we aren't girls. We're nothing." They didn't dwell on the unpleasant. But Lena's attitude was different from Zina's.

The first time she was told that she was beautiful, she just sniffed and wheeled herself away. And she had snubbed the head teacher, Mikhail Ivanovich, when he had said those same empty words to her. "You can't walk with your face! Give me a pair of legs!" she had snapped at him and then muttered for others to hear, "Clumsy bear." And that had become the old man's nickname. A half hour later Lena had gone to him to apologize. He had waved it off, shaken his head, and said diffidently: "It was my own fault, Lenochka, forgive my stupidity." Still, it made her feel bad.

But what was the good of being beautiful? It would be easier on her if she were downright ugly—then everything would match. And so Lena avoided mirrors.

But now she went close to the mirror and stared at herself. First angrily. Then with a smile. And finally with tears in her eyes.

But these were not tears of bitterness, for they brought her a strange sense of relief. She dried her eyes and continued to stare calmly at herself. Well, the braids were all right, golden. And the eyes, all right too, nice and big. But that was only because she was skinny. Her face wasn't bad. What else? Arms and hands, just like everyone else's. Anything else? No, nothing.

She wheeled herself angrily away from the mirror, again thinking that being home was having a bad effect on her. Those stupid tears. The mirror. No, being home alone wasn't good for her. Definitely no good.

Alone? But what about Fedya? Why did he blush when he talked to her? And he hadn't gone back to the pigeon cote for the rest of the day or even passed by her window. Had he been hiding at home? But then, why had he walked past with his father?

A bunch of stupid questions! She picked up a book. She read a few pages and then realized she was just making her eyes move and couldn't remember a word of what she'd been looking at. She switched on the TV. A soccer game. Big deal—running around and kicking a ball. She switched off the TV and picked up her transistor radio. After a mishmash of voices and languages she found some music. A boy was singing: "Round is the sun, blue is the sky." Old stuff, she thought, and tossed the radio onto her bed. No, she'd go crazy here. Soon she'd be getting hysterical. She had to get back to boarding school. It would be awful to be alone for a whole year, to miss a year of school just because she'd had pleural pneumonia. So what if she had? Why did they worry about her? Even if . . .

She struck her fist painfully against the arm of her chair. Again. And again for all her idiocy. All those ideas about life beyond the grave. Better to think— all right, so I go back to school, to the girls. But Fedya, what about him?

Hmmm, Fedya. What did he have to do with it? What had come over her? Suddenly she turned her chair and wheeled herself back to the mirror.

"Well now, Helen the Fair," she said, "have you really gone and fallen in love?"

She moved away quickly, went to the TV, and switched it on full blast. Then she turned on her radio and found some blaring jazz. She snatched up a book and started reading aloud at random, shouting at the top of her lungs.

" 'The moon hung low in the sky like a yellow skull,' " she screamed. " 'From time to time a huge misshapen cloud stretched a long arm across and hid it. The gas-lamps grew fewer, and the streets more narrow and gloomy. Once the man lost his way and had to drive back half a mile. Steam rose from the horse as it splashed up the puddles. The side-windows of the hansom were clogged with a grey-flannel mist. "To cure the soul by means of the senses, and the senses by means of the soul!" How the words rang in his ears! His soul, certainly, was sick to death. Was it true that the senses could cure it?' "

Lena screamed the words, straining her voice. Thousands of fans at the soccer stadium roared from the TV, and the radio was still blasting away. Now she felt better.

Suddenly her mother's face was in front of her. Her eyes were blinking rapidly. She caught a glimpse of her father's gray temples. He was moving swiftly about the room turning off the television and the radio.

"What's wrong?" he asked sternly, frightening Lena. She had never been afraid of anyone in her life, she didn't know what fear was. But there she was, scared.

"Oh, nothing," she stuttered. "Oscar Wilde. 'To cure the soul by means of the senses and the senses by means of the soul.' "

Still blinking, her mother felt her forehead. Lena laughed.

"His soul was certainly mortally ill. But was it true that the senses could cure it?"

"That settles it, I'm quitting my job," said her mother.

"Nonsense," Lena replied calmly. "A person has a right to have some crazy moods. Just ordinary crazy moods. Nothing so terrible about that."

Her mother went off to the kitchen, but her father remained with her. Suddenly he knelt down in front of Lena's wheelchair and began kissing her hands. She tried to pull them away. She couldn't understand what was going on.

"Lena! What's wrong?" she heard her father's desperate cry. "What is it?"

Lena managed to pull her hands free and pressed her father's head to her.

"I'm sorry," she said. "Did I frighten you? Of course. What a fool I am."

He rose from his knees and moved toward the corner of the room. "We bought you a dress. A long one," he said with forced gaiety.

Lena clapped her hands in delight. "Don't show it to me now. A bath, first a bath!"

That was her own ritual—a bath before trying on anything new. And at home there was another ritual—her father was the one who bathed her.

They had started that when she was a small child and there was nothing to be shy about. Her father would pick her up and carry her to the bathroom. He would roll up his sleeves, put on his wife's apron to protect his pants, then soap and rinse her as carefully as any mother. Lena never felt shy with her father. Maybe that was because she never felt more an invalid, more inferior, than when she was undressed.

But now all of a sudden she felt shy. For the first time ever.

Her father filled the bath, put on the apron, rolled

up his sleeves, and went to get Lena. But she was still sitting there fully dressed. She glanced up furtively at him. He understood.

"All right," he said. "Your mother can do it."

Lena closed her eyes. Something had definitely happened to her on that crazy day.

"Wait," she whispered. "It's all right."

She took off what clothes she could herself, and her father helped her with the rest. Then he picked her up, light as a feather, carried her to the bathroom, and gently lowered her into the warm water.

The water somehow made her feel like herself again.

"I'm sorry," she said. "Something's not right with me."

"It's nothing." Her father smiled. "You're just growing up."

"Growing up?" she said in surprise, and took cover under the water.

For a while neither of them said anything. Water dripped merrily from the faucets. Her father took three small brightly colored ducklings from the shelf and dropped them into the water. He had been doing that for as long as she could remember.

"The ducklings are still little," said her father gently, "but our Lena's growing up."

"Dad!" she said abruptly, and her eyes filled with tears. "Dad!" she repeated. "Tell me, what's the good of my growing up? Look at me. I can feel that I've gotten bigger, there's some kind of force working on me from the inside. On my breasts. My hips, my shoulders. But for what? What's the use of it? Look at my legs. They're good for nothing. They're just two sticks."

"Stop that!"

"Wait, Dad," she said, brushing away a tear. "Be patient with me. Just a little more patience. Help me. Give me an answer. What am I growing up for? A woman is born to have children. But me? I can never be a mother. I must never love anyone. And nobody will ever love me, do you understand that? Then what's it all for?" Lena fell silent, glanced over at her father, and slid under the water.

"My daughter," he said, taking her wet hand in his. "At every moment someone is leaving this life. And sometimes death is a release from suffering." He paused. "If I were a religious man, I would say—let us pray. But instead what I say is—let us believe. Believe in ourselves, in our own strength. Believe that we are human and that you are a person, not a big person yet but brave and wise. You can do anything. Always remember—it's easier not to be than to be."

Lena looked up at him, her eyes open wide.

"Dad," she said, "I believe you, I really do, only it doesn't make things any easier for me."

For a long moment he sat on the stool swaying from side to side.

"It would be wicked to lie to you," he said finally. "Things won't get any easier for you."

He straightened up and began washing her, rubbing her hard yet tenderly; she helped him or rather helped herself. Then, all of a sudden, her heart grew bright and clear again.

They didn't talk anymore. Her father wrapped her in a large Turkish towel and carried her to her room, then helped her on with the new dress and in braiding her hair. Lena's mother was in the kitchen making supper, and so the whole sacred ritual had occurred without her.

When everything was complete, her father pushed Lena's chair in front of the mirror and called her mother. Her mother looked at Lena and sighed with pleasure. She saw a grown-up girl in a long lilac dress with a bright floral pattern that went wonderfully well with her blue eyes, the golden braid tossed over one shoulder, and the crimson flush of her cheeks.

7

Fedya waited for his father to notice how neat and clean the room was and to give some sign of his approval, but he seemed to be blind to it all. He paced the room from one end to the other, sometimes fast, sometimes slow, as if he couldn't keep still. It didn't feel right to Fedya to put on "The Waves of the Amur." All right, he thought, I'll wait till Ma comes home.

But she was late. And Fedya and his father felt ill at ease with each other. Neither of them spoke, as if there were nothing for them to talk about. His father kept pacing nervously and blowing smoke out the window. Finally he said, "Maybe I'll just pop out for a few minutes."

Fedya shrugged. He couldn't hold his father by

force. He could go if he wanted. But once he went out, those old buddies of his would be right there, and then it would start all over again. . . . "Wait a little while, Dad," Fedya pleaded.

His father grunted, sat down at the table, and pushed away the vase of flowers, wrinkling the table-cloth. He picked up the newspaper.

Fedya understood what was wrong with his father, why he was gruff and restless—he wanted a drink.

At last the door opened and Fedya breathed a sigh of relief. He ran to the record player and turned it on, then he ran over to his mother and grabbed her shopping bag from her.

"Come on now, time to dance."

His father and mother just stood there staring at each other as if they'd just met. His father's arms were trembling; his fists hung heavy as stones, as if he couldn't unclench them. His mother frowned, her shoulders sagging like an old woman's. She smiled a timid sort of smile.

"Well, come on, you two." Fedya laughed. "Dance!"

But by this time the music had stopped. Fedya made a gesture of annoyance.

"What's the matter with you, forgotten how to dance? You used to be able to."

"It's been so long, Fedya," said his mother. "But look at the room, it's so clean and tidy, it's beautiful. You did a great job, son."

"It wasn't me," Fedya said, shaking his head. "It was Dad."

"Him?" she said with a laugh. "Are you kidding?" She cut herself short with a quick glance at her husband, then sighed deeply.

"What about me?" said Fedya's father morosely. "Think I can't do it? Think I can't be relied on?"

It hadn't worked, it hadn't turned out right at all.

"Forget it," broke in Fedya. "Let's have some supper."

He ran to the stove, broke some eggs into the frying pan, plugged in the kettle, set out the dishes, and began slicing the bread. His parents sat idly at the table, exchanging an occasional uncomfortable glance but not saying a word to each other.

"You know, Ma," said Fedya, just to say something, "you know that tumbler, the one with the biggest crop, well, his tail's been pulled out. Some cat must have got up onto the roof. And, Dad, could you get someone at work to set my hacksaw? You've got men there who know how to do that, don't you."

His parents mumbled a reply, but then suddenly his mother said, "You see, Gera, it looks as if we've forgotten how to live like normal people. We can't find a thing to talk about unless we're drinking."

She went to her shopping bag and pulled out a bottle. Fedya threw his knife angrily on the floor.

"What kind of people are you? Do you mean that you can't even talk without drinking?"

He was shaking with fury. His mother! Yesterday she'd been saying she wanted to leave, couldn't stand any more, and now she brings home a bottle. The light and color went out of everything, the room he'd taken so much trouble over, the whole wonderful day.

Smoke was rising from the frying pan. Fedya grabbed the pan, banged it down on the table, and started for the door.

"Where are you going?" cried his mother.

"To hell with both of you!" he said, his voice choked. "Stupid people!" He slammed the door behind him so hard that bits of plaster fell from the ceiling.

Night had fallen, a dark, dark blue. The stars were out and it was very quiet.

Fedya walked fast, hot with rage.

He thought of the day that had just ended. But not of how it had ended. He thought of the pigeons in the clear sky, the curtain at the window, Lena's face. Her face rose before him, obliterating all else. Her enormous eyes, the braid wound around her head.

There was something about her, something mysterious, something about the way she looked at him—maybe that was what had him spellbound, her way of looking at him.

Fedya walked to his pigeon cote and raised his head. Lena's curtain was lit by a warm rose-colored glow. He could hear the sound of faint laughter. There you see, he thought, everything's fine up there. They're probably sitting at the table, she and her parents, drinking tea and making jokes. While over at my house . . .

Anger suddenly flared up in him again. How would it all end? Would it ever end?

His fists clenched, his fingernails digging into the palms of his hands, as he thought of his own mother and father. He'd have to fight. Something had to be done, and if his mother was no help, he'd have to find a way.

Fedya glanced up at the warm rose-colored window again, then turned and set off at a run. He burst into his apartment with such force that the door banged against the wall, startling his parents, still sitting at the table. The bottle was almost full. Fedya grabbed it and threw it out the window. A moment later there was a muffled crash.

"That's that!" shouted Fedya. "Now you can beat me. Or kill me!"

But his parents remained motionless. Fedya looked at their glasses—they were full. So they hadn't drunk anything. And the eggs were cold. Something strange was going on. And he had no idea what it was.

Suddenly his mother burst into tears. His father moved closer to her and began stroking her back.

"We're in deep trouble," she sobbed. "What's going to happen now, Gera? What's going to happen to Fedya?"

"Don't worry about it yet," said his father.

"*Now* what's the problem?" cried Fedya in desperation.

His mother shook her head and covered her face with her handkerchief.

"There's been an audit at our warehouse and I'm short," she said.

In a fury, Fedya shouted, "You mean you're a thief?"

His mother took the handkerchief from her face and looked him straight in the eye. "How could you even think that? I've been so upset lately, I must have been careless. I must have made a mistake in counting and somebody took advantage of it."

Fedya looked long and hard at his father.

Now look what's happened.

Now look what you've gone and made her do!

8

The evening had been quiet and warm, but morning brought a lashing rain. Lena was worried—Fedya probably wouldn't come, he wouldn't be there humming that little song of his. Even the pigeons were quiet. Either the rain was drowning out their cooing or they were quiet because of the bad weather.

Raindrops struck her window and ran together in larger streaks. Occasionally someone would hurry past, wearing a raincoat and carrying an umbrella, then the street would become deserted again.

Her dress looked beautiful on its hanger. Lena had asked her mother not to put it away in the wardrobe, and whenever her eye lit on the lilac material with its colorful patterns, a smile would come to her lips.

If only the girls could see her in it! She'd give anything to wear it to one of their school parties.

They had parties quite often at the boarding school. Vera Ilyinichna said they had more parties than regular schools.

The entire school community would assemble in the auditorium, teachers and nurses too. The stage was never used. How would they have gotten up onto the stage? They would sit or lie on the floor or stand in a circle. The headmistress or one of the teachers would make a few introductory remarks, then ask if anyone would like to perform.

There was a really gifted girl, Zhenya, a pianist. Like Lena she was confined to a wheelchair. She would wheel herself over to the piano and play a few simple pieces. They were proud of her, and the entire school would applaud her wildly. They had a rule—nobody was ever made to perform and nobody had to prepare or rehearse any "numbers." The parties often lasted until after midnight. They recited poetry and prose—and they also liked to listen to records, everything from big band and pop opera to Tchaikovsky and Beethoven. Everyone had a good time. They all liked to see dancing. One evening when the headmistress was new, she had put on a record and announced a waltz. A few of the girls who could move about fairly well took a whirl at it, but when one of the girls fell, the dancing was stopped. After that, the only dancing was done by teachers and visitors, and the students enjoyed watching them, applauding after each dance. The teachers felt embarrassed, Vera Ilyinichna especially, but the children insisted, so now all their parties ended with the teachers dancing.

Those parties were the main event at boarding school. The girls looked forward to them, dreaming of something new to wear. Those parties were both their main distraction and a kind of test for them.

Lena had memorized a large number of poems by Pushkin, and at one party, especially arranged for her, she challenged the others to guess who had written them. She recited for a whole hour. Then at the end, when Vera Ilyinichna placed a laurel wreath on Lena's head, she told the audience that all the poems were by Pushkin.

They clapped wildly, applauding Pushkin—and Lena for her amazing memory and her knowledge of the classics. When the applause had died down, Lena read another poem. This poem had a special meaning for her.

"When in my arms your slender beauty
  Is locked, oh you whom I adore,
And from my lips, between the kisses
  Love's tender words delight to pour,
In silence from my tight embraces,
  Your supple form you gently free,
And with a skeptic's smile, my dear one,
  You mockingly reply to me;
The sad tradition of betrayal
  You have remembered all too well;
You listen dully, scarcely heeding
  A syllable of what I tell.
I curse the zeal, the crafty ardors,
  I curse the criminal delight
Of youth, and the appointed meetings,
  The garden trysts in the hushed night;
I curse the whispered lovers' discourse,
  The magic spells that lay in verse,
The gullible young girls' caresses,
  Their tears, their late regrets I curse."

Lena's face was flushed when she finished reciting. The applause was especially wild, and there was a strange, half-happy, half-sad expression on everyone's face.

Now Lena imagined herself sitting among the boys and girls in her wonderful long dress reciting those poems.

She had all sorts of fantasies. To be a pilot. To fly a supersonic plane. Or to have an amazing voice that could reach every register, to stand on the stage of the Bolshoi Theater, the boxes glittering, the audience entranced. Or to be on skis, shooting down a steep mountain slope—everyone else falling down, even the tall, athletic men, but Lena flashing past, the wind blowing around her strong, beautiful legs.

Oh, all those fantasies and dreams! She could only whisper them to Zina or to her other friend, Valya. Only they could understand her, her and her dreams that had nothing to do with life, real life. One day Zina, wheeled her chair up to Lena's and said conspiratorially, "Listen, this is by an English writer and scientist, C. P. Snow. 'The individual condition of each of us is tragic. Each of us is alone. Sometimes we escape from solitariness, through love or affection, or perhaps creative moments, but those triumphs of life are pools of light we make for ourselves, while the edge of the road is black: each of us dies alone.' " Zina read it all in one breath.

"Do you understand? Do you get it, Lena? They know about everything in the world. Even death! And here's us making up stories and fantasies. We make up pools of light, we read books, and discuss things. But in reality we're alone."

Lena disagreed, and yet she copied Snow's words

in her notebook. And learned them by heart.

On days when their spirits were high, Lena would lean close to Zina's ear and quote Snow's melancholy words, and they would burst out laughing—the somber thought wouldn't seem so somber anymore. On the contrary, it would sound absurd. What would life be without love and affection?

"All that's easy for healthy people to say, but that's not for us," said Valya. She was the only one they had told about the quote from Snow.

9

Lena parted the curtains and caught sight of Fedya's face. He was sitting inside his pigeon cote. Even though the rain could not reach him there, all the same he looked like a drowned rat. Lena smiled and opened her window.

"Don't pigeons fly in the rain?" she asked.

"No," he said, his teeth chattering.

"I don't see your logic then."

"What?"

"The pigeons aren't flying but you're sitting in there."

"I just felt like it."

She wanted to tell him to come up, but the thought frightened her and she even moved away from the window. So far he had seen only as much of her as showed through the window, but if he came up he would see all of her. Her new dress caught her eye, and suddenly she knew why she had wanted it.

Lena went back to the window. "Will you count to three hundred?"

"And then?"

"And then take a handful of wood shavings and come up. We're on the third floor, the first door on the left."

She closed the curtain so as not to see the expression on his face.

For a moment she sat without moving, her hands dangling. Then she wheeled herself over to the long dress and began unbuttoning her blouse. It wasn't easy for her to change her clothes. At school Nurse Dusya had helped her, and some of the girls had given her a hand too, and her parents helped her at home. Taking off the blouse was simple. The hardest thing was to get out of her skirt and into her dress. To do that she had to raise herself up on her hands, first on one, then on the other.

She was excited and hurrying. While Fedya was counting to three hundred in the pigeon cote, she went through the numbers mentally herself. They had their own special games at school, some of which were quite serious. One of them was changing a dress without help before you counted to three hundred. Lena had been able to do that at school. But that had been her record, and done under very different conditions. There had been no real hurry. No date waiting for her.

A date? She laughed while supporting herself on one hand and shoving the dress under with the other. The chair slid backward and Lena, caught off balance, fell to the floor.

She had every right to cry, but she laughed instead. Using her hands, she crawled over to the chair. The pretty new dress picked up dust as she dragged along the floor. She grasped the wheelchair and tried to pull herself up. The dress caught on something and tore a little. What a pain, she thought.

The chair defied her and rolled away under her weight. She had nothing to brace herself against. In the end she dragged herself up on it by sheer strength alone.

Fedya was ringing for the fifth time now. She straightened out her dress hastily and tidied her hair. Then she wheeled herself quickly to the door. She laughed again. A date!

Lena could feel that her laugh was unnatural. Her

heart was racing, beating like a heavy hammer. She took a deep breath and opened the door.

Fedya stood there, dumbfounded. He looked at her legs and at the wheelchair. Then after a polite greeting he came in and removed his boots.

"Did you break your leg?" he asked, crossing the room. "I was in a cast all last summer. I fell on my arm. They put braces on it—they looked like the struts they used to have on the old-fashioned planes."

He was very talkative and seemed not to be giving her a chance to answer.

"No," she said. "I have no legs."

"What do you mean, no legs? There they are, I can see them."

"They're there and they're not." Fedya saw her turn pale. "I can't walk."

He opened his mouth to say something, but Lena cut him short. "Don't you dare pity me!"

Fedya looked at her, utterly lost, his green eyes growing darker by the minute. "And there I was yesterday envying you all like a fool," he said.

"Why, you think there's nothing about me you can envy? You think I'm just a useless invalid, a sad cripple. Oh mister, can you spare a few kopecks?"

She wasn't shouting. Her voice was icy, each word clipped.

Not knowing what to do, Fedya squeezed the shavings in his hand.

"Should I leave?" he asked softly.

Lena stopped short, gave Fedya a searching look, and nodded.

"Yes. Go."

He laid his shavings on the table, pulled on his boots, then turned to Lena. She was sitting in her wheelchair, her head straight, looking out the window.

Fedya closed the door carefully behind him.

Rain was still lashing the ground, flattening the grass and whipping froth on the puddles, but Fedya didn't run or look for shelter. He walked slowly, as if he were unaware of the downpour, saying to himself, "Of all things, of all things."

The image of the helpless girl in her wheelchair filled his mind. He was confused as to how long he had been at Lena's. A minute? Two? They had said a few words and now it was all over. He'd never visit her again, never talk with her again. Maybe it had been his own fault. Of course he'd been startled by that wheelchair. And her saying she couldn't walk. Maybe he'd gaped and stared at her, but that wasn't so terrible, was it? It was the first time he'd seen all of her. He had a right to stare. But then he'd said that thing about envying her. He hadn't meant any harm by it, he'd been thinking about his own troubles that came down on him the way wormy apples get blown off an apple tree. And she?

She'd been thinking about herself. Only about herself, and her own troubles. And they had blotted everything else out. She just hadn't understood him. And right away she had started defending herself. By attacking him.

Fedya went home and lay down on his bed, wet as he was, but then he jumped up and changed his clothes. He lay down again. Outside, the world was bare and gray and he felt the same way inside. He'd gone to the pigeon cote just to see her. But now how could he go back there? Knowing she was watching him. He just couldn't go back to fly his pigeons as if there were nothing wrong.

He could have pretended there was nothing wrong and said, You're wonderful. Don't think about your legs. Good legs, bad legs, what's the difference? He could have said that, but it would have cost him his self-respect.

Fedya opened a magazine, read a few lines, then closed it. It made no sense.

He had been so critical of his parents lately. They couldn't understand each other and didn't even want to try. His father's drinking had made his mother so miserable that she had gone and gotten herself into trouble. She looked terrible, yet his father never even noticed. Maybe it was the same with him and Lena. Maybe she thought Fedya was glad she had problems too, and glad there was nothing to envy her about. But could she really think that?

Fedya paced up and down the room until a puzzling thought made him stop short. He was acting like his father. Feeling mixed up. He'd acted like a fool. A ninny. Goddamnit, it was all his fault. A sick girl was sitting up there all alone. She'd felt sorry for him and invited him up, and all he could say was that he shouldn't have envied her. Idiot!

He leaned his hot forehead against the window, which was pleasantly cool. He ought to go back to her. It was so stupid! He should apologize, say something, do something.

Fedya put on his raincoat, slammed the door, and ran down the steps. The rain was worse than before, the nearest buildings scarcely visible.

Fedya ran headlong toward Lena's house when he stumbled and fell, almost knocking Lena out of her wheelchair.

"Where are you going? Are you crazy?" he cried, staring at her in disbelief.

"To see you. And you?"

"To see you."

Lena, her face wet with rain, was wearing her father's waterproof cape. Her long dress was soaked to the knees, and her hands were muddy to the elbows from turning the wheels.

"How did you get down?" asked Fedya. "How did you manage the stairs?"

"Fedya, I'm a fool, a tremendous fool!"

"Me too," he yelled happily. "An even more tremendous one!"

They laughed until they were doubled over. A good thing there was no one around—people would have thought they were crazy.

Still laughing, Fedya bent down and tucked the rain cape around Lena's legs, placed her hands under it as a joke, then turned the chair around and sped it back toward her house.

They only stopped laughing when they reached the front hall.

"Aha!" said Lena. "I got down by holding on to the banisters. But how'll I get back up?"

Fedya felt quite confident now. "Give me your key," he said.

He ran up to third floor, opened the door to Lena's apartment, and then came back down.

"Put both your hands around my neck."

"But they're dirty." Lena laughed.

"Do it!"

She clasped her hands around his neck and said softly, "I hear and obey."

Her voice whispering in his ear and her hair tickling his cheek gave Fedya a sort of funny feeling. He smiled, picked her up, and carried her upstairs. She was very light, which made him feel all the stronger.

"You're crazy," he repeated as he climbed the stairs. "Just plain crazy. Down those stairs in a wheelchair. And then out into the rain!"

He took the stairs one at a time, mumbling foolish words to Lena, who had grown very quiet. A warmth rose in his throat and his heart glowed with tenderness.

"Crazy," he said again. "Completely nuts."

He carried her in and set her down on the sofa. When he stepped back, he saw that Lena was pale, her eyes closed.

"Hey, crazy one!" he called softly to her. She did not respond. Alarmed, Fedya said it again, louder this time. Again no response. Fedya began to feel panicky.

He looked around, searching for medicine, or anything that might help, then he bent down close to her face to listen for her breathing. Reassured, he moved back a little. Suddenly, without opening her eyes, Lena said, "Kiss me!"

"What?"

"You idiot," she said, her eyes still closed.

Silently he knelt down and touched her warm, moist lips with his.

"You smell like wood shavings," she whispered and opened her eyes.

"And you smell like rain," he said and kissed her again.

She put her arms around his neck and they kissed again, eagerly and clumsily. They floated off in a cloud where the window's gray wetness seemed to sparkle with sunlight, until suddenly Lena cried out: "The chair!"

The wheelchair was still down in the front hall, and the door to the apartment was still wide open. With some difficulty, Fedya rose from the floor and, smiling foolishly, left the room.

He brought the chair back up, locked the front door. Lena had put the wet raincape on the floor and was now facing away from the door.

"Lena!" whispered Fedya as he moved closer to the sofa.

"What got into us?" she asked, shaking her head. "It was like an eclipse."

"There's going to be a real eclipse tomorrow," Fedya whispered. "An eclipse of the sun." Lena nodded after each sentence. "I'll come for you. We'll watch the eclipse together."

He kissed her again. She did not pull away, but when he drew closer she held up her hand.

Her hand was dirty from propelling herself through the mud. Fedya took her dirty hand and pressed it to his cheek.

His eyes burned with delight as he looked at her. Calmer now, Lena smiled back serenely at him.

10

Lena's mother didn't notice anything. Fedya had straightened up the apartment, wiped clean the wheelchair, and carefully ironed the dress and placed it back on its hanger. But Lena couldn't hide anything from her father.

The first thing he discovered was a wood shaving. He picked it up and asked her where it came from. She had to tell him about Fedya. He didn't say anything, but later she caught him looking uneasily at her a few times.

As if possessed, Lena began belting out the first song that came into her head, "The Young Eagles Are Learning to Fly," then switched her radio on to Tchaikovsky's "Sentimental Waltz" and waltzed her chair around the room, unable to keep up with the beat but panting and breaking her fingernails from trying to. And when she caught the smell of wood shavings in the air, her eyes grew larger and silly giggles escaped from her lips.

She recited Pushkin to her mother and father, the same poem she had ended her recital with. It had a new meaning for her now. To avoid betraying what she felt, Lena played with the poem, exaggerating her tones and expressions, but at the same time watching her parents' reactions.

> "I curse the zeal, the crafty ardors,
>   I curse the criminal delight
>   Of youth, and the appointed meetings,
>   The garden trysts in the hushed night."

When she finished, her mother applauded, but her father sighed.

"All right," he said, "you've fallen in love. I can understand that. Introduce me to the young man."

"I will. Tomorrow. By the way, there's going to be an eclipse tomorrow."

"A what?"

"A solar eclipse. We're going to watch it together. How do you watch a solar eclipse, Dad?"

"With a special astronomical device, I guess. What is he, an astronomer?"

"Of course," she said quite seriously. "An astronomer, a philosopher, an expert on pigeons, and lots of other things too."

Her father walked over to the window rather quickly, looked out at the pigeon cote, and whacked his forehead.

"I should have guessed. So, it's Fedka. The American's son."

"His name is Fedya, not Fedka. And I don't care if his father is a Martian as long as it doesn't rain tomorrow." Lena laughed.

The weather was glorious the next morning. It was a Saturday, and Lena's parents didn't have to go to work. Lena was worried that Fedya might get intimidated and not come to see her.

She wheeled herself nervously about her room, listening for every sound from outside—Fedya just might signal to her from the pigeon cote. But Fedya had not let himself become intimidated. When the bell rang, Lena made a dash to the door, but her father was there before her.

Fedya stood in the doorway looking well dressed in a white, short-sleeved shirt and well-pressed trousers. There was a hint of a future mustache above his lip, and the lock of black hair, which he was always shaking back into place, had fallen onto his forehead.

"Good morning," he said cheerfully, and stepped in without waiting for an invitation.

Lena's mother began to blink rapidly as she tried to decide how she should act. Ill at ease, Lena's father began coughing.

"I know you already, more or less," he said. "Your name is Fedya."

"And you are Pyotr Silich."

"Well, now you've introduced yourselves," Lena laughed, seeing her father smile with relief. After all, what had happened? A friend had come to see her, and that was no reason for her father to start coughing or her mother to have a blinking fit. A world-shattering event! Her father seemed to have reached the same conclusion.

"What are you going to watch the eclipse with?" he asked Fedya.

Fedya smiled and took something neatly wrapped in newspaper from his pocket. He opened it, revealing two pieces of ordinary glass that had been smoked over a candle.

"With these," said Fedya, smiling shyly.

"God, how simple!" marveled Lena's father. "I thought you would need some sort of equipment.

We live in such a complex world, we forget the simple things!"

Fedya felt ill at ease and glanced at his watch. Lena's father began to clear his throat.

"You know," he said, "Lena hardly ever gets outside. Let's take her down into the courtyard so she can watch that eclipse of yours from there."

"Why is the eclipse mine?" asked Fedya, smiling shyly again.

Lena's father seemed embarrassed again—he coughed and apologized as he and Fedya carried Lena outside.

When they were alone, Fedya sighed loudly. The wheelchair was right beneath Lena's window near the pigeon cote. Her parents looked down at them from time to time, but still, they were alone.

Lena's legs were wrapped in a warm plaid blanket, and she was wearing a wool jacket even though the sun was still very bright.

"And yesterday you rushed out into the rain with only a dress on," he said reproachfully. "If your parents only knew!"

There was still a little time before the eclipse, and so Fedya went up to the cote and let his pigeons out. They soared up into the sky, and Lena, her head tilted back, her eyes narrowed, watched their exultant flight.

"It's wonderful!" she said.

"I love them."

"I didn't mean the birds. I meant things in general. It's wonderful to be alive. Even if you don't have legs."

Fedya gave her a stern look. "Why talk about that?"

"Why not, Fedya?" she said with a smile, and then softly, "Kiss me! I'll keep an eye out for them."

She glanced up at the window. Fedya kissed her near the ear.

"Not like that," she whispered.

"How?" he asked, surprised.

"Better. Like yesterday." She took his hand, aware of its roughness. "Fedya, it's all so silly. Yesterday after you left I started having daydreams like a little fool. But then I thought—well, all right, let it be. Kissing may be sad, but it's nice too."

"Why sad?" asked Fedya.

"Because there's no sense in it. It's all just for now. I had a little luck, that's all. You'll meet a normal girl and then you'll forget all about me."

Fedya didn't answer; he watched his pigeons in their flight.

"Did you hear what I said?"

"I never thought about that."

"Well, you'd better."

"I don't want to," he answered quickly.

Lena looked at him. So that's what you're like, she thought, you don't want to. But you're going to have to. She was about to say that but changed her mind. He's right not to want to, she thought. I don't want to think about it either.

The pigeons circling in the endless sky suddenly seemed to stop, and swooped down all at once. Something had upset them. They flashed past Lena and Fedya like pale shadows, flew into their cote, and began cooing in alarm.

"Here," said Fedya, and handed her a piece of smoked glass.

Lena shut one eye, but then realized she could look through the glass with both eyes open.

Seen through the piece of smoked glass, the sun looked like a well-polished five-kopeck piece—copper red, and very close. The sun warmed their hands, though the glass made it look cool.

Fedya glanced at his watch.

"It's time," he said. "watch closely."

At first Lena didn't notice anything. Then the edge of the sun began to grow uneven, as if a piece had been gnawed off. And slowly it began to look more and more like the moon.

The wind had died down, but Lena felt cold and

began to shiver. Fedya looked at her in surprise—
her teeth were chattering. He put down his piece of
glass and took her hand. It was as cold as an icicle.

"What is it?" he asked, worried. "What's wrong?"

But Lena could not tear herself away from her
glass; the darkening sun held a strange fascination
for her.

"It's nothing. Look! You're missing it!"

Dusk fell quickly. Frightened crows cawed franti-
cally in the poplars. Then the sun vanished. Its place
in the clear blue sky was taken by a black disc. The
pigeons cooed shrilly in fear.

"Fedya," whispered Lena, "I'm frightened."

He took her hand again.

"Hold on," he said. "It's almost over."

The black disc hung in the sky for another moment, then one edge of it turned silver. As though
relieved, the breeze sprang up again. The sky grew
lighter. Slowly the sun freed itself from the terrible
shadow until it was copper red again. Lena tossed
her piece of glass aside, but she kept looking at the
sun, whose brightness stung her eyes to tears.

Now the cooing of the pigeons had a soothing
sound to it, and the crows in the poplars stopped
cawing. Lena felt warmer. She turned to Fedya, who
was looking at her with panic in his eyes.

"What happened to you?"

Lena shrugged. "Something."

"I'm a fool. I shouldn't have brought you out here."

"Yes, you should have," she said, breathing a sigh of relief. "It's good to be alive. And to look at the sun. If you want to understand anything, you have to see the darkness cover it. Do you know what I mean?"

For a long time neither of them said anything. The wind stirred in the dry grass, rustling the bushes and the poplar leaves.

"Problems are like eclipses," said Lena. "But life is the sun."

Just then Lena's father came out and joined them. He asked Fedya to show him one of his pigeons.

Fedya climbed quickly up to the cote, and returned with a wary red tumbler, which he handed to Lena. The bird squinted at its new mistress, then glanced questioningly at Fedya. It opened its beak, showing its sharp pink tongue, and blinked comically.

Lena listened as Fedya explained to her father about the pigeons, but none of it made any sense to her. Fedya wasn't listening to himself either. He was looking at Lena. And Lena was looking at him.

II

Fedya called himself every name in the book. His mother was in serious trouble, and all he could think about was Lena. Lena's face was always before him—his own happiness had shunted his family problems off to one side. He had stopped thinking about his father altogether. That was thoughtless, but then, there was nothing he could do about it. He remembered only when he was walking in the door.

On Friday his father had made it home on his own, sopping wet but sober. He had stayed home Saturday. His mother was at the warehouse, where they were finishing up the audit, but his father stayed in, gloomy as a thundercloud.

When Fedya came home, he couldn't believe his

eyes. There was his father, barefoot, wringing out a wet rag as if he hated it, making the rag squeal. His face was fit for a funeral as he slapped the cloth down on the floor. He was cleaning up the place! Unbelievable!

"I'm not the bum you think I am," he said, and went on working on the floor.

Fedya shifted from one foot to the other, not knowing what to do. He couldn't go into the room, and it'd be stupid to go back to the pigeon cote. He'd just said good-bye to Lena. She'd be glad to see him, but what would her parents think? He turned around and set off to see his mother at work.

The fruit and vegetable warehouse where she worked looked like a factory. It had a guarded entrance gate and row upon row of gray buildings with trucks rumbling by, the loaders shouting—it was a noisy place.

The empty warehouse, its gate wide open, looked like a dark gigantic mouth. A cold, raw, rotten smell came from inside it.

Fedya went in. It was gloomy and deserted. An unpainted stool glimmered faintly in the dim light. Wearing a black smock and boots, his mother sat on the stool with only her face and hands visible. There was something eerie about the stool, the face, and the hands against the black background. Her hands were pressed against her face.

For a moment Fedya thought of sneaking up on her and surprising her, but something made him decide against it. His mother was swaying back and forth on the stool as if she had a toothache.

Fedya squatted down in front of her and said, "Take it easy, Ma, it may all be okay."

"No, it won't," she said, choking on her tears. "They've already counted everything up, and I'm short seven hundred rubles. I've got a week to make good on it or else they'll take me to court."

"Good!"

"What are you so happy about?"

"Because now we know where we stand. Seven hundred rubles—we'll scrape it together somehow, borrow if we have to. If you want me to, I'll sell the pigeons."

She took his head in her hands, and as she looked into his eyes, her own filled with tears again. Then she pressed his face against her black smock.

"Oh, my son, my wonderful son, what would I ever do without you? I'd go hang myself, that's what I'd do."

Fedya pulled himself free of his mother's hands and shook his head with displeasure. "Don't talk like that!" Then he thought of his father. "Look at Dad, he hasn't had a drop for three days now, and today he was washing the floor."

"No!" She laughed. "You're joking."

"No, I'm not. He was whacking the rag so hard, the water was shooting out of it."

She laughed again and then began to cry again. Fedya patted her head and tried to convince her to quit her job altogether. She could find something better.

"But the seven hundred rubles, Fedya, it's no joke. Seven hundred rubles is a lot of apples and peaches and grapes! And those men, that commission, they way they looked at me! She stole it, they said, that's all there is to it. But some good people stood up for me too."

Fedya nodded and listened, cursing himself because here was his own mother telling him her troubles and he couldn't get Lena out of his mind—he kept seeing her eyes, her hair, her lips. His mother's troubles just seemed to drift away from him, and didn't touch him no matter how much attention he tried to pay to them.

"Look, Ma," he suddenly found himself saying, "don't worry. Did you know there was an eclipse of the sun today?"

"So?" she said indifferently.

"The sun disappeared, and everything went all dark and eerie."

"And so?"

"Your troubles are like a solar eclipse," he said, smiling at the thought of Lena. "It won't last long. And then the sun will come out again. It's already out—you just haven't noticed."

His mother sighed, pulled out a handkerchief, wiped her eyes, and stood up. She shut the warehouse door and locked it with a huge padlock.

"How'd you get so smart?" she asked. "All those eclipses."

Fedya laughed. "I learned."

"Who from?"

"Good people."

"Are there any?"

"You just said so yourself—good people stood up for you."

She nodded in agreement.

"Bad people took advantage of me, but good people stood up for me. I just wonder if they're not all the same though, the good and the bad."

Fedya didn't really understand what she was saying and didn't make much of an effort to, either. He was thinking of Lena again and how she had turned cold as ice when the sun had disappeared.

Everything was clean and tidy at home. His father was sitting at the table wearing a white shirt, his hair neatly combed, his face clean-shaven. Fedya wanted to say something, but he couldn't, not with his father's gray-haired childhood friend Ivan Stepanovich sitting across from him and a quarter-liter bottle with a red label on the table between them. The bottle hadn't been opened yet, but you could snap off the cap in one second. Fedya and his mother both frowned. Seeing them frown, Ivan Stepanovich asked with a sigh, "Tonya, what have you done to John? For the last hour I've been trying to tell him it's Saturday and we've got to celebrate. But he doesn't want to. He seems pretty solemn to me."

"We've got plenty to be solemn about and nothing to celebrate," said Fedya's father with a downcast look. "Well, how'd it go, Tonya?" he asked his wife.

She burst into tears and told them about the seven hundred rubles. Ivan Stepanovich snapped the top off the bottle, poured himself a shot, and drank it down. Then he cleared his throat, to reassure either himself or all of them, and said, "In for a penny, in for a pound." Then he rose and walked out without another word. Fedya's father shrugged his shoulders, watching his friend go.

"Well, now," he said. "Let's take a good hard look at it all, Tonya. Don't lose heart, seven hundred rubles isn't all that much money. We'll figure something out."

He went to the wardrobe, opened the creaky door, and took out his good suit that he had hardly ever worn.

"Here's the first hundred."

Fedya's mother sat down on the edge of a chair and Fedya stood silently behind her, smiling happily. That was the kind of father he'd dreamed of. They could call him John or the American or even Uncle Sam, he wouldn't give a damn. He hadn't touched the vodka even though his old buddy had tried to talk him into it. Now he was acting and speaking with a quiet assurance.

"What about the record player, Fedya, can we stand to live without it?"

"Sure we can!"

"Well, that's another fifty. And Tonya, where'd you hide my rifle? It's a good thing you did. I should have sold it a long time ago—I'm no hunter. That should be good for another hundred and fifty."

Excited by his father's actions, Fedya came out from behind his mother, took his new pants, shirt, and nylon jacket from their hangers, and tossed them on top of his father's suit.

"How much are they worth?"

Then Fedya's mother got up and began taking her dresses off their hangers, but his father took her by the arms and made her sit down. He put her and Fedya's things back, a stern look on his face.

"It's my fault, and I'll be the one to pay for it. You two take it easy."

Fedya's mother began crying again. His father sat down beside her and made an awkward attempt to comfort her. "There, there, Tonya, what's wrong?"

"Gera! Why couldn't you always have been like this? And not broken my heart with your drinking?"

He lit a cigarette, his hands shaking, and said hoarsely: "I quit! I promise! I swear it! That's it!" He burst out laughing. "I'm as good as the next man. We'll go to movies, we'll have fun together. We can even go to the theater."

He put his arms around his wife, grabbed her hands, and whirled her around the room, knocking the vase of flowers to the floor.

Fedya laughed happily, for they say a broken vase means good luck. The eclipse was over, the sun was shining again.

Life was strange. When everything had been all

right, they had been miserable, but now their troubles seemed to have woken his father up.

His mother was laughing. His father joined in with his own scratchy laughter. Fedya stood smiling, watching his parents. None of them noticed the men standing in the open door. His father's old buddies—gray-haired Ivan Stepanovich, Platonov, and bald Yegor.

Fedya's spirits plummeted. It was obvious they'd come looking for his father. They were half drunk already—the stink of alcohol filled the room.

Then his parents saw them. His father let his mother down carefully and said to them, "Nothing doing. I quit."

Without answering him, they came in and sat down at the table.

"Well, shall we finish it off?" said the gray-haired one. "It's a sin to let it go to waste."

They poured the vodka into a glass, which they then passed around, each one taking a sip. Fedya's parents stood by the table staring in surprise at their uninvited guests, trying to fathom what was going on. But Fedya understood. These were his father's tempters, his Mephistopheles.

He was ready to tell them to clear out and never come back, to let him and his parents alone, not to interfere in their internal affairs, as the newspapers like to say. He was just about to launch his attack when Ivan Stepanovich patted down his gray hair and nodded to Platonov. "Well, get on with it."

Platonov rummaged in his pocket and pulled out a handful of crumpled bills. "There's a hundred here," he said in a rasping voice.

"The price of a case." Yegor sighed.

"A case of what?" asked Fedya's mother.

"You know."

"Cut that out," said Ivan Stepanovich, cutting him short, and then he announced ceremoniously: "Gera, accept this from your old friends. You too, Tonya. Every little bit helps."

Now all three were exchanging happy glances and clearing their throats. Fedya felt his own throat constrict with emotion. He'd been on the verge of calling them a bunch of drunken bums and kicking them out. And look what they'd come up with! And they even seemed embarrassed about it.

Fedya's father hugged them and pounded their backs so hard you could hear it, and they pounded his. Fedya's mother had started crying again, wiping her tears away with her hand because her handkerchief was already soaking wet. First she'd cry, then she'd laugh again.

Someone knocked at the door and the room went silent. The smiles still on their faces, everyone turned toward the door.

Fedya held his breath as the door opened. Lena's father, Pyotr Silich, was standing in the doorway. He nodded and then, embarrassed, coughed into his hand.

"I've brought some money," he said.

"But we don't know you," said Fedya's father.

"Yes, we do," said Fedya, blushing and thinking of Lena's face, her big eyes and golden hair.

His father's old buddies turned toward Fedya as if they'd just noticed him. His parents were staring at him too. There was some sort of suffering written on his mother's face, a painful memory having just crossed her mind.

12

At first Lena had taken them for drunks getting together over a bottle. She had gone to the window and carefully pulled the curtain aside. "If we let John's Tonya go to jail, we'll have to live with that the rest of our lives," said the man with gray hair.

They were standing by the pigeon cote, money rustling in their hands.

"Remember Tonya when she came here, Ivan? When they got married? Just a lanky long-legged kid, and now . . ."

"That goes for all of us now," said the third man, and patted his friend's bald head.

They all burst out laughing. Lena realized what they were talking about, and she was angry with Fedya for not telling her about it. Even those drunks were collecting money to help out Fedya's mother, so how could she just sit by and do nothing?

She wheeled herself away from the window and called her father. He came into the room, his glasses low on his nose, a newspaper in one hand, and looked inquisitively at her.

"Dad, Fedya's got a problem, but he didn't say a word about it to me. His mother was short at work or something like that. He needs money."

"How much?"

"I don't know."

Lena knew her father would understand. He left the room, and a few minutes later he came back dressed to go out. When her mother heard what was happening, she blinked and nodded her head.

"Of course, no question, we have to help. But who are those people? We don't even know them."

Lena rolled her eyes.

"You remember Fedya, don't you? It's his mother," Lena's father said, and left.

Her mother wheeled Lena over to the sofa and sat down, the two of them alone together. It was then that Lena realized how much more time she spent with her father than with her mother, who seemed always busy in the kitchen. Someone had to cook of course, but still . . .

"Lena, my dear," said her mother stroking her hand, "this may make you angry, and your father wouldn't agree, but maybe it would be better not to . . ."

"Not to what?"

"Not to get too friendly with that boy, that Fedya."

Lena felt like smashing something or shouting at her mother, but she restrained herself and only asked, "Why not?"

Her mother seemed embarrassed. "Well, you know, he's quite different from you. I mean he has a different kind of a life, flying his pigeons and all."

"You mean I can't fly pigeons? Well, all right, I can't. So what?"

Lena found her mother's constant blinking thoroughly annoying.

"You have your own friends," added her mother hastily. "There's Zina, and the other girls in your dormitory. And there are boys in the boarding school too."

Lena understood what her mother meant, and oddly, she was neither angry nor offended, only sorry for her. Her mother was trying to protect her again, to see that nothing happened that could hurt her later on. Lena held out her hand, and her mother reached eagerly forward. Lena held her close and patted her head as if her mother were a small child.

"Don't worry," whispered Lena. "I know."

"What do you know?" asked her mother, moving a little away.

"I know I've got to expect disappointment, hurt, loss."

"No, no," cried her mother with obvious falseness, "that's not what I was thinking about."

"Then what?" asked Lena.

"Well, all right then, if you insist. He won't understand about your illness. He won't understand that you and he are different."

"That's enough, Mother," said Lena, growing angry. "That's just another way of saying the same thing."

At that moment the doorbell rang. Lena's mother went to open the door, expecting her husband. But Lena heard a woman's voice, a very familiar voice.

"It's my class mother!" cried Lena, wheeling herself toward the door.

Vera Ilyinichna came into the room with flowers in one hand and a cake box in the other, both of which fell onto the sofa as Lena flung her arms around her teacher's neck, squealing with delight.

"Let me get a good look at you," said Lena. "That hairdo—you must have spent a good two hours at the hairdresser's! But you've got dark circles under your eyes. Still plenty of worries, I see. . . . How are all the girls?"

The girls! It was only when her class mother arrived that Lena realized that she'd totally forgotten about the girls. When Fedya had come into her life, she had forgotten everything else—school and all had just slipped right out of her mind.

"Oh, Mom," cried Lena, "I want to go home, back to school to see everyone!" But her eyes were laughing and she wasn't really missing anybody and didn't really want to go back to school at all—there'd be no pouring rain there, no pigeons, no Fedya, no kisses, no eclipses, no intoxicating aroma of wood shavings, no kindly drunks coming to Tonya's rescue.

"That's not true, Lena," said Vera Ilyinichna. "There used to be a time when you could fool me, but that time is past. I can tell by your eyes. I can also tell that you've got plenty of news."

"Tons!" cried Lena. Her mother sighed as she picked up the cake box and flowers from the sofa.

"Well, I'll leave you two," she said sadly. "I'll put the flowers in water and make some tea, but first I want to ask you a question, Lena: Why do you call me Mother and Vera Ilyinichna Mom?"

Lena did call her mother "Mother" sometimes, with a hint of irony in her voice, an irony she did not bother to conceal. It was only now that she could see that. She remembered how her mother always blinked when talking with her, and suddenly all that seemed horrible to her, truly disgusting. She had always taken pride in not exploiting her condition, the way some people did, turning it into a sort of advantage. But the way she talked to her mother, that stupid, unnecessary irony, that condescending tone—it was disgusting because her mother couldn't answer it, because Lena was her daughter, her invalid daughter.

Kindness, that was it, that was the only thing Lena wanted now. All she wanted to be was infinitely kind and good. Always, everywhere, and to everyone. Especially to her mother. The woman who had given birth to her. Given birth to her in pain. Ugly and helpless as she was. But in her mother's eyes she was beautiful.

"Please come to me, Mother," said Lena, tears welling in her eyes.

Her mother bent down and Lena hugged her. And with the other arm she hugged Vera Ilyinichna.

"It's because I love you both," said Lena. "And because I understand you. And you understand me. We understand each other. After all, we're all women, aren't we?"

What had come over her? She never used to be able to stand anything that smacked of sentimentality, and now here she was, sniffling with her mother and Vera Ilyinichna and then bursting into laughter because it really was comical, that trio of sniffling noses. She laughed and the two women laughed with her. Lena began besieging her class mother with questions: What had the latest parties been like, what was the latest school news, was Zhenya still playing piano, and, most important, what was happening with her group and especially her dorm?

"How's Valya?"

"She's embroidered another rug."

"Great! And Nurse Dusya?"

"She's either napping or complaining."

"And the headmistress?"

"She put up a hundred jars of strawberry compote for New Year's. It'll be a real feast."

"And Zina?"

"She's all right."

"Is she learning her poetry?"

"Yes."

Lena looked at Vera Ilyinichna in surprise—her face had gone tense for an instant but then relaxed again. She started asking Lena questions, about her health and the books she'd been reading.

"I've been reading *The Picture of Dorian Gray,* by Oscar Wilde, and there's one scary line in there— 'To cure the soul by means of the senses, and the senses by means of the soul.' "

Vera Ilyinichna smiled. "And what about 'the criminal delight of youth'? Isn't that the same sort of thing? Pushkin was pretty adventurous too, you know."

"Today there was an eclipse of the sun, did you know that?" Her class mother's expression changed again, but Lena didn't wait for an answer. She was dying to talk about Fedya. Her voice dropped to a whisper. "A boy showed me the eclipse. His name is Fedya. We watched it through pieces of smoked glass. And do you know what?" said Lena, squeezing her teacher's hand. "I felt so cold, I was just frozen."

"You too?" cried Vera Ilyinichna, startled.

"Yes. Were you cold too?" But Vera Ilyinichna didn't answer Lena's question, and Lena was glad to continue. "Dad just went over to Fedya's to help his mother. Some money is missing where she works."

"Helen the Fair," said Vera Ilyinichna, "have you by any chance fallen in love?"

Lena became very still and then nodded her head, saying eagerly: "Yes, yes, yes, yes!"

Vera Ilyinichna moved a little away, looked curiously at Lena, and then moved closer again, but she didn't say anything.

When Lena's father returned, they had tea and cake. Lena was aware of Vera Ilyinichna's eyes on her, but she would look away whenever Lena glanced in her direction.

Something was wrong. Maybe she thought the same as her mother. But Vera Ilyinichna did not always look away, and Lena's eyes would meet their warm brown glow, their clear smile, and feel that her teacher did not condemn her. It was something else she was concealing.

When Vera Ilyinichna was leaving, Lena's mother saw her off. She didn't know that anything said by the pigeon cote could be heard in their apartment, and it was there she stopped to talk with Vera Ilyinichna.

"You know," she said, "sometimes I feel that Lena is older than I am."

"Me too," replied Vera Ilyinichna. "And maybe it's true. You know, at first I felt lost with them at the school. It's nothing like a regular school—the children at the boarding school have a heightened sense of truth, even if it's painful and hard to bear."

"Sometimes that honesty frightens me." Lena's mother sighed.

"You shouldn't be frightened of it. You must remember that in a school for sick children there is no room for lies."

"Listen to them philosophize down there," Lena told her father. "As if they could not have said all that up here. Please shut the window."

But before he shut it, Lena heard Vera Ilyinichna say, "But Lena—she could have been a heroine, like Ulyana Gromova or Lyubov Shevtsova. She has such tremendous potential. Such great spirit!" She paused and then said, "It's so unfair!"

Lena's father shut the window, and turning laughing to Lena, he said, "Now there I don't agree!"

13

On Monday Fedya woke up with a vague sense of
alarm, which remained even though his parents left
for work happy because everything was all right and
his mother had the money to repay the shortage at
work. But all the same Fedya had an uneasy feeling
in the pit of his stomach that morning. As he lay
there in the quiet of the room, he heard a muffled
rumbling coming from outside—it sounded as if a
truck were stuck in the mud and couldn't get out.

Fedya got out of bed, washed, and went outside.

Although autumn was a good way off, the prickly
grass and the dusty path were already beginning to
be littered with poplar leaves. There was no wind;
the sun shone palely in the washed-out blue of the
sky, while the dusty acacias that separated their little

enclave from the noisy streets hung limp and gray. Still, the air had a countrylike fragrance of its own. The smell of grass mingled with the acrid aroma of the phlox flowering in the tiny gardens.

Fedya heard another rumbling sound, which made him feel uneasy again. The noise wasn't coming from the city streets—it was coming from somewhere past the neighboring barracks. Fedya followed the sound till he came to a tumbledown two-story barracks like his own. Standing next to it were several trucks. Nervous and excited, people were carrying out their possessions and loading them onto those trucks. A bulldozer rumbled nearby.

Down the street a number of men with surveyors' poles and theodolites were moving with an unhurried, confident, businesslike air.

Fedya noticed the bald head of his father's old friend Yegor in the lively crowd around the trucks. Fedya slipped nimbly past the trucks, tables, and sideboards until he had reached Yegor.

"We're all through here," shouted Yegor, wiping his bald head with a handkerchief. "We're moving into a new building."

"All of you at once?" asked Fedya, surprised.

"That's right. They're tearing everything down.

They're moving everybody out. You too. There's going to be a high rise here, a hotel or something."

Fedya watched the people scurrying about, dragging their possessions. It reminded him of ants whose anthill had been knocked over. Now he knew why he had been feeling so uneasy.

He went over to one of the men with theodolites, a young man with a mustache who would wave one hand, then the other, then jot something down in his notebook. He gave Fedya a sort of superior look.

"What's going up here?" asked Fedya.

"A square. A fountain. Flower beds with Dutch tulips. We're replacing those shacks with a hotel, a movie theater, and a supermarket. It'll be really something to look at! Why are you looking so glum? Everybody else seems happy about it."

Even old bald-headed Yegor, who had lived here all his life, was glad the old barracks were being torn down. In a new building he'd have an apartment of his own and not have to share the kitchen and bathroom. The only problem, Fedya thought, was that people wouldn't know each other. They'd all use the same front door, but they'd all be strangers. There were two boys in Fedya's class who had lived in the same sixteen-story building for a year before they discovered they were neighbors.

Fedya walked along the road looking at the trailer

trucks that had brought in the earth movers and bulldozers. He watched the huge trucks belching dark-blue exhaust fumes as their rumbling filled the street. This made him feel even worse.

He ran to his pigeon cote.

His pigeons' cooing had a free and happy sound to it—he wasn't late today, but he hadn't brought any food with him. The birds cocked their heads and looked inquisitively at him, but Fedya's mind was far away.

What was going to happen now? To the pigeons? To Lena? And to him?

Lena's curtains stirred and opened slightly for an instant, and then a paper bird came flying out. It swooped down and struck the ground. It was immediately followed by another, then another, and yet another.

Fedya felt a sudden rush of tenderness for Lena. She must have spent the whole morning making those paper birds so she could have her own flock to fly.

He smiled when Lena opened the curtains wide and, laughing, started sailing her paper pigeons right at him. Some of their paper beaks caught on the cote's metal netting. Fedya pulled them out and sailed them back to her.

"Everything's going to end soon," he said.

"I know," said Lena, and Fedya was stung by her light and casual tone.

"They're going to tear this whole place down," he said. "They've already brought in the machines."

"And what's going to be here?" asked Lena, her voice quivering.

"It's what won't be here that matters. My pigeon cote won't be here, and your house, and my house, and this street, and the acacias."

"What'll happen?" she asked flatly. "To us, I mean."

Her words struck Fedya like a blow. That's what had been troubling him all along. At first, it had been unconscious, just a premonition, and then it had grown clearer, but he still hadn't been able to put it into words. He felt so bad about losing their little enclave, his pigeon cote, even their old tumbledown house that he could have wept. But they weren't the most important things. What mattered most was Lena. What was going to happen with them? With them!

He opened the cote and the pigeons soared up into the sky, vanishing in the sun's pale rays, reappearing as snow-white or red points against the blue of the sky.

Now that they were alone, they could have talked

and laughed, but they didn't say a word and kept avoiding each other's eyes. Just as if they had quarreled.

"I want to see it," said Lena at last, and Fedya climbed down from the cote. Again he carried her downstairs, and again her hair tickled the side of his face, but he did not kiss her this time. And neither of them broke their silence.

The tires of her wheelchair sank into the dust as they went, and passersby cast them sympathetic glances. They still weren't talking, still acting like strangers.

The dump trucks were still roaring and people were still carrying furniture out of Yegor's barracks. Nothing had changed and yet everything had changed.

Fedya wondered if Lena hadn't believed him and had wanted to see for herself.

They didn't stay there long. Half an hour later they parted without saying more than a few words to each other. Fedya climbed back up to his pigeon cote and called his birds in for the day.

On his way home he turned several times, hoping to catch a glimpse of Lena's face, but her curtains were drawn.

14

Lena couldn't understand what was happening.

She had spent the entire morning making paper pigeons to make Fedya laugh, but when he told her the news, something within her seemed to break.

She became numb, stony, lifeless.

What would become of them now?

Lena had known what would become of them— she had known the end would come even without dump trucks and bulldozers. She had thought she was prepared for everything, and was ready to accept whatever happened, no matter how bitterly disappointing it was.

But she had thought it would happen slowly. That they would part gradually, over a period of time. When a person is happy, it is hard for her to believe that that happiness will ever end.

Unlike Fedya, Lena had had no premonitions, no feelings of alarm.

She had made her paper pigeons while listening to the real ones coo. Waiting for Fedya to appear, she had smiled in anticipation of sailing the whole flock down at him at once. But then it had felt as if everything had run into a brick wall. And when he had come up to carry her downstairs, she had wanted to sob, to howl from the despair of knowing that they only had a short time left together.

She had remained silent, her heart beating with dull monotony. If Fedya had tried to kiss her, she would probably have turned her head away.

After Fedya left, she drew the heavy curtains, closed her eyes, and let her head fall back against the headrest of her chair.

Could it all really happen so mercilessly?

To level and destroy it all—their houses, the pigeon cote, the whole little cluster of houses! And then build some stupid hotel complete with fountains and flower beds!

She could picture the water splashing in that cold concrete fountain. That water would have no life to it—its sound would be flat and meaningless as it fell against the concrete. Only what is alive can feel and suffer, and only something that is devoid of life can flow on calmly and not grieve for what has once been there.

A dead fountain with dead water as in a fairy tale, and lifeless crimson tulips swaying lifelessly in the breeze.

And no pigeons. Their place in the sky would be taken up by skyscrapers. And no poplars, only dead thick grass. No Fedya, no Lena. As if they had never been there at all.

Then why was she even bothering to sit here and think about things that soon would be no more?

Lena circled the room in her chair, telling herself, Ideas, it's all just ideas. But she couldn't stop herself. She brought herself to an abrupt halt. Were all those ideas coming to her because she was sick, crippled, abnormal? Was the rush of thoughts and ideas besieging her because she was damaged, defective? It was something she had never wanted to admit, something she feared and rejected.

Lena tried to sort things out and put them into some sort of perspective. The pungent smell of wood shavings, reading Oscar Wilde aloud with jazz blaring and the soccer fans roaring. Tears, kisses, and the solar eclipse when her heart had seemed to stop. And then today that numb feeling . . .

Nothing like this had ever happened to her before. Never!

There had always been a healthy atmosphere at school. Strict, spartan rules. An iron determination not to give in to your illness had produced the unwritten laws they all observed. And no one had observed those laws more faithfully than Lena.

Perhaps it was too much freedom that was to blame? Freedom, being alone, being away from the "community," as they called it at their meetings, a community that might not be strong and healthy in the literal sense of the word but which was nevertheless strong in spirit.

There were times, she remembered, when one girl or another would break down. But that didn't happen very often. And all the other girls would give her their full support. When you're part of a group, stumbling isn't so dangerous, the others won't let you fall.

But now she was alone.

Face to face with herself. With Fedya. With everything that had been happening. And it was breaking her, bending her, twisting her.

Lena laughed, remembering how Vera Ilyinichna had said she could have been a heroine like Ulyana Gromova or Lyubov Shevtsova.

Nonsense. Empty words. Impossible.

Lena circled the room again, then leaned wearily back in her chair and closed her eyes. She fell asleep suddenly, as if falling into a dark pit.

15

Everything became hectic.

It seemed hard to believe that their old neighborhood, with its dusty paths, the smell of grass, and the rustling poplars, had once been as quiet as the country. It was like a great anthill that had been disturbed, and apparently no one had realized there were so many creatures living there. People began moving to new buildings on the outskirts of the city, and yet their numbers never seemed to decrease. Mass confusion broke out in the enclave, the sort of urgency you might expect on a sinking ship.

Then, one evening, Fedya's father received the papers for their new apartment. He had taken a drink that day, but neither Fedya nor his mother noticed—they were much too stunned by the news.

Fedya had been hoping against hope that somehow they would be skipped, their house would be left standing and everything would stay the same. But they had not been skipped, their house would go, and nothing would stay the same.

His parents wanted to see the new apartment immediately, and naturally Fedya had to go with them.

"Don't take it so hard, son," said his mother on the bus. "You were talking about selling your birds anyway."

Fedya sighed and nodded. His mind whirled with confusion. But more than anything, he felt crushed by Lena's terrible indifference.

Fedya had been up to see Lena several times that day, both during the day when no one else was there, and in the evening when her parents were home. Lena had treated him like a casual acquaintance. She would move away when he tried to come close, and once she had wheeled herself away so fast that her chair had crashed against the wall. Her eyes were empty and glassy when she looked at him.

Their new apartment was on the outskirts of the city, on the tenth floor. But being on the tenth floor did not mean, as Fedya had expected, that they had a view of the forests reaching off into the distance.

No, their building was surrounded by monsters that were sixteen and twenty stories high. So all you could see was the sky above and the empty, resonant well, formed by the other new buildings.

But his mother was as happy as a little girl. She turned the faucets on and off, tested the shower, examined every detail of the electric stove, and leaned so far over the balcony that she frightened Fedya's father, who ran over to her and grabbed her by the waist.

"It's lovely!" she cried. "And look, not a single beer stall."

That brought a grunt from Fedya's father. "You want me on the wagon for the rest of my life?" But he was smiling too as he went from room to room, measuring the lengths of the walls.

"If they're giving me a place like this, they must think I'm worth something. True or not?"

"Of course, of course!" Fedya's mother laughed. "You can do anything you want." And then she added jokingly, "It's just getting you to want something that's the problem."

Two big, airy rooms, a kitchen, a bathroom, and an indoor toilet! There'd been nothing like that in the old place—there you could only dream of such things. And of course Fedya was happy too—it was just that, thank God, he had not reached the age when material things could obscure the more important things in life.

Now there were new sounds in their old neighborhood, great crashing sounds that fascinated Fedya and drew him like a magnet.

It was a crane swinging a great iron ball on a cable. The crane operator would raise the ball, turn the crane slightly as though taking aim, and then swing the huge ball against some rickety wall.

Cracking and groaning, the walls would collapse, revealing sad and empty rooms that had been people's homes for so many years. With a pang of sorrow Fedya noticed on one wall a cheap color print in a frame—forgotten, or perhaps just abandoned. In another room an army cot, stripped of sheets, and on the windowsill a geranium in an old blackened clay pot, its leaves fluttering.

Fedya was having the same nightmare night after night—he would see naked-looking chimneys and a latticework of windows with the panes banging in the wind. Then he would hear the dull thud of the iron ball smashing the walls of the old houses, and he would shudder to think that soon it would be their house's turn to collapse like a sick horse sinking to its knees.

But he was never to witness that.

He helped his parents move the furniture to the new apartment; then while his father hurried back with the truck, he and his mother unpacked. Darkness was falling when they returned to the old neighborhood, without quite knowing why they'd gone back. But by then it was all over. Their old house was a mound of rotted timbers, tufts of wadding, and shattered plaster.

Standing beside the ruins of their house, Fedya's father happily told them that he had talked the crane operator into letting him knock the building down himself. Fedya could not understand his father's glee—why had he wanted to knock down his own home?

Fedya felt a warm affection for the old house; he felt as if a living creature had been killed.

He had moved away into the gathering darkness and headed for the pigeon cote.

All the windows in Lena's building were brightly lit. As if everything that was happening around the building were of no concern to the people inside. As if their building, taller and better than all the barracks, could expect to last forever and rest secure.

Fedya did not climb up to his pigeons. He had fed and flown them during the day, his eyes constantly looking up to Lena's window. But there wasn't a sound from her place. Finally, despondent, he had left to help his parents load the furniture. She must have seen the truck go past her window, but she didn't even part the curtains as they drove away to their new apartment.

Now, in the darkness of the evening, Fedya put his foot cautiously on the first rung of the ladder. He could see Lena's shadow on the curtain. She was reading. He could feel his heart beating fast and felt an impulse to call out to her. A strangled sound came out of him, but he stifled it.

The shadow moved—Lena must have heard him. Fedya froze.

In anguish Fedya realized that today he had lost his home. That soon he would be losing his pigeons. And he was also losing Lena. Lena! Lena!

16

Lena knew Fedya had come back to his pigeons. She heard his stifled sound, almost a choked sob, but she gave no sign of herself. She had watched everything, of course. She had seen him load the furniture and drive past her window, his eyes looking right at her, but not being able to see her behind the curtains. And she had seen Fedya's father attack their house until the glass and plaster went flying.

Everything seemed to have dried up in Lena, like a brook during a heat wave. All her juices, all her kindness, all her eagerness for life, sank beneath the surface where no one could see it. Even her face became sharp and dry.

"You have to break it off with Fedya," she told herself. "Do it. It's best that way."

Lena's illness had taught her to be harsh with herself. In the evening when her parents were home, she would pretend to be happy, smiling and joking; she would hide in the bluish glow of the TV, pretending to be absorbed in the program.

She had to end their relationship. Soon her father would be getting the tenancy papers for one of the new apartments, and that would be it. The end! And then she could breathe freely again. She had to be strong. Her illness had taught Lena to overcome any obstacle. Sorrow. Unhappiness. But why couldn't she overcome happiness? That should have been simpler.

When she heard the bell ring, she was sure it was Fedya. Lena wheeled herself to the front door. But when she opened it, she saw a postwoman whose frown changed to a smile when she saw Lena.

"I've got a registered letter for you."

Lena scribbled her signature in the receipt book, thanked the woman, closed the door, and returned to her room.

The envelope was marked "Personal."

It was from Valya.

Dear Lena,

Even if you were very sick, you can never be forgiven,

she read.

We know that Vera Ilyinichna went to see you, but you never came. And Zina was so fond of you. Always remember the day of her death, Saturday, the day of the eclipse. And let that day weigh on your conscience forever.

Lena gasped for breath. There was a faint ringing in her ears that grew louder with each second. Using all her strength, she made herself exhale and dropped the letter on the floor. Lena was shaking, close to convulsions. She tried to cry but couldn't. She felt as if she were afloat on some bottomless sea of horror with no shore in sight. All she could do was thrash helplessly about—it was senseless to try to swim, there was nowhere to swim to.

Zina dead? Impossible! Why? How?

Zina had suffered so much. Her left arm and leg had been paralyzed. Once Zina had said, "It'll be easy for it to get me!" "What do you mean?" Lena had asked. Zina laughed. "The paralysis. All it has to do is go up or down a little and it's right here," she said, pointing at her heart. Could she really have known what was going to happen to her?

But Vera Ilyinichna! How could she? She knew Zina and Lena were friends. Why didn't she tell her Zina was dead?

Why? How could she be so cruel?

Lena tried to recall every detail of the visit. Had she said anything unusual? Yes, she had mentioned Zina, but then they had talked about the eclipse. Lena had told her how cold her hands had gone and about the chill that had gone through her. It was then that Vera Ilyinichna had turned pale and said, "You too?"

But Lena had paid no attention to that remark. That day the whole world was beautiful to her and she had not paid much attention to Vera Ilyinichna's words. "You too?" Had she been referring to herself? No. To Zina.

At last Lena burst into tears. Valya had written that Zina had died on Saturday. Vera Ilyinichna had come the same day. But why had she come? She must have come before the funeral. Had she come to tell Lena? So she could come to the funeral? But she hadn't said a word about it. How could she? How dare she?

Lena threw on her coat and wheeled herself to the stairs. Clinging to the banister with both hands, she lowered herself down the stairs, one step at a time.

Her chair was not designed for street use—it had no levers or brakes. Slamming the front door behind her, Lena wheeled herself past the acacia trees and out to the busy, noisy street. She was oblivious to everything around her. Including Fedya, who watched her rush past him.

"Where are you . . . ?" But she didn't answer. Just kept going, leaving Fedya standing by the side of the road with a look of confusion on his face.

Lena wheeled herself into the middle of the busy street. She knew she should have kept to the sidewalk, but it was too crowded, and she could make better time on the road. She kept the wheels spinning, staring straight ahead.

Cars jammed on their brakes and went carefully around her; some of the drivers stared at her in disbelief. Lena remembered that she had no money with her. She realized she could stop a station wagon and have herself, chair and all, loaded into the back where the luggage went.

She began to laugh hysterically.

Luggage! That's what she was. That's what Zina had been. And Zhenya too. They were all luggage. Things, inanimate objects that could easily be transported in the luggage section of a station wagon.

The street began going downhill, but Lena didn't notice it, and kept pushing the wheels. A few times the hard tires struck her hands painfully, but she paid no attention. Her chair began picking up speed, the spokes were humming, the wind was racing through her hair. Suddenly Lena saw she was heading to the left side of the road, right at the oncoming traffic.

It all seemed somehow ridiculous.

Lena grabbed hold of her knees, making no attempt to steer the chair away from an oncoming bus that was drawing closer and closer. When the driver saw her, he braked sharply and brought the bus to a screeching halt. Lena could see the even rows of rivets on its blue side. She leaned back and shut her eyes.

"No!" she screamed.

She heard a faint *clunk* and suddenly the chair slowed down. She felt it going up onto the sidewalk and come to a stop.

When she opened her eyes, she saw Fedya's agonized face before her.

"What are you whispering?" he asked. "What?"

But she hadn't been whispering, she'd been screaming—"No! I don't want to!"

Fedya didn't ask any more questions. Slowly, he

walked to the back of the chair and asked her calmly, "Straight ahead?"

"Yes, straight ahead," she said.

They came to a stop in front of the cemetery.

"Why here?" Fedya asked.

"I have to go in there."

"No."

"Let me go in," she commanded.

"I won't."

Lena turned around quickly, her eyes red.

"You have no right to stop me. Zina is dead!"

She hid her face in her hands. Lena shuddered as the chair began to move. She heard a brass band playing inside the old cemetery's wrought-iron fence.

They were playing a funeral dirge.

Fedya stopped again.

Zina must be buried close to the new grave where the brass band was playing. There was no sense in Lena watching the funeral. Better to wait. Fedya wheeled her quietly along the wrought-iron fence.

Autumn had begun its implacable approach. The ground by the fence was covered with a carpet of red and gold leaves. They rustled underfoot and gave off a heady aroma. The sun was still warm.

Fedya winced, thinking of what might have happened had he given in to his hurt feelings and walked away when Lena ignored him as she rushed past him.

She'd be in the hospital now, or dead. He would never have forgiven himself. It was a good thing he had followed her.

It hadn't been easy, for she'd been going straight down the road at terrific speed while he had to run down the sidewalk, dodging people as he went.

Fedya had seen the chair pick up speed as it rolled downhill, then swerve out of control, heading straight at the oncoming bus.

He had heard the squeal of brakes, he had seen people stop to watch him race past and grab hold of the chair when it was about six feet from the bus and push it up onto the sidewalk.

Another moment, another couple of seconds!

The music stopped and Fedya started slowly toward the cemetery gates. The musicians, carrying their gleaming instruments, laughing and talking, were followed by the silent funeral party. As Fedya and Lena passed through the gate, some of them stopped and stared at them.

Fedya wheeled Lena along the tree-lined paths. Birds were singing gaily among the leaves, and the sun, penetrating the treetops, lit the gravestones like a spotlight. The cemetery struck Fedya as artificial, unreal, as if it had been expressly designed to frighten people.

Zina's grave was at the end of a row. The freshly turned earth of the neighboring graves was of various colors, fresh and brown on the newest ones, but grayer and drier on the older ones. On Zina's grave the earth was already hard and gray.

Lena huddled in her chair, covering her eyes as her shoulders shook with silent sobs.

Her weakness and helplessness awoke tender compassion in Fedya and gave him strength and confidence. He sat down in front of Lena and firmly removed her hands from her face.

"Lena!" he said. "Lena, remember! Try to remember what you told me. About the eclipse. All our sorrows are eclipses, but they are a part of life. Without them you'd forget how to see the sun!"

Lena looked at him, absently at first but then with some recognition of what he was saying.

"You know what Zina once found in a book?" she said slowly. "Listen." Lena took a deep breath, as if throwing off a burden, glanced quickly again at Zina's grave, and then looked searchingly at Fedya. "Listen," she repeated. " 'The individual condition of each of us is tragic. Each of us is alone. Sometimes we escape from solitariness, through love or affection or perhaps creative moments, but those triumphs of life are pools of light we make for ourselves, while the edge of the road is black: each of us dies alone.' "

"Is that from the Bible?" asked Fedya.

"No, it's by C. P. Snow. Ever hear of him?"

Fedya shook his head.

"Well, that's Zina now," she said. "Alone."

"Enough of that," said Fedya. Lena did not argue. He turned the chair and began wheeling her toward the gate. Fedya felt relief when they had left the massive gate behind them and were back in a street vibrant with life—a bus went honking past, a mutt ran by yelping.

In the cemetery Fedya had felt power and ascendancy over Lena, but that had lasted only a brief moment. Now he was at a loss for words again.

What was it she'd said? Pools of light we make for ourselves.

"You know," said Fedya, "that C. P. Snow of yours—he contradicts himself."

Lena didn't answer.

"Love, affection, and what else was there? Anyway, you have to create them. Yourself. He said so himself."

Lena kept silent. Fedya felt anger rising in him. He swung her chair around and faced her.

"It's true what he says about the pools of light, that Englishman of yours. But a person is a thinking creature. If a person recognizes that loneliness is inevitable, that means it's in his power to turn his life into one great pool of light!"

"But Zina's dead!" Lena wept. "And I'll die too."

"We all will. So what should we do then, just lie down and die?"

"No, Fedya," she said. "Some people can never understand each other. In our school we have no time to think about pools of light." She thought for a moment, then added, "It's not for us to be creating any pools of light."

"Who put all that nonsense in your head?" cried Fedya. "You're rejecting who you really are. You're a strong person, I've seen it, I know. There are plenty of healthy people who are worse off than you! What if they all gave up? What if they all just thought about dying all the time?"

People stopped to look at them, but Fedya was completely unaware of them. He felt an overwhelming tenderness for Lena. His heart ached with pity for her, and the more helpless she was, the greater his love grew for her.

"Today's just an eclipse!" he said, gasping for breath. "Just think of it like that—an eclipse. See, your hands are cold, just like they were then. Wake up! Look around! Remember what Ostrovsky wrote, damnit—we've only got one life, so live it! Live!"

Fedya felt that he was on the verge of tears. He swung the chair around abruptly and began pushing it. He was crying silently, biting his lips to prevent any sound from escaping, and running as fast as he could, the wind whistling in the chair's spokes. He was crying in despair, at not being able to make Lena understand and overcome her grief. But at the same time he could feel his own grief and anger rising in him.

Anger at the bulldozers rumbling in their little enclave behind the thick wall of old acacias, at the cranes swinging the iron balls against the sides of houses. The old was being destroyed to make way for the new.

But the new does not always bring joy with it. And it is hard to lose the old. Especially when it has been part of everything you loved.

17

As soon as Lena saw her parents and Vera Ilyinichna running to meet them, she remembered the letter she had dropped to the floor as she rushed out of the apartment.

Her mother shouted at Fedya, "Why did you take her there?"

But her father said calmly, "Thank you for not leaving Lena."

Fedya did not say a word.

Lena looked at Vera Ilyinichna. She had to ask her something, and yet the longer she looked at her, the less she felt like asking.

What had Vera Ilyinichna hoped to gain by saying nothing? Lena would have learned of Zina's death sooner or later. It was a mistake done out of kindness. She had been too compassionate and had put off telling Lena. Spared her for a time.

Lena remembered when she told her about Fedya and answered, "Yes, yes, yes, yes!" when her teacher asked her if she was in love. She was happy and everything seemed so wonderful. Why condemn Vera Ilyinichna? For being kind? Then what was there to ask her about?

When they reached the front door, Lena heard Fedya say, "Good-bye."

She turned her chair to face Fedya. He was standing about ten feet away. His hair looked very black, and he was wearing a light-colored shirt and faded jeans. His eyes looked very tired and his hands hung limply at his sides. Lena shuddered as if someone had cracked a whip beside her ear. Now she understood. She had lost Zina. But now . . . now Fedya, who was real and alive, was drifting away from her.

"Fedya," Lena pleaded. "Fedya, what's going to happen now?"

"I'll come see you," he said, moving away. "Don't worry, I'll come."

He turned and ran as Lena moved the chair quietly through the door. Then she was lifted by her father's strong arms and floated up the stairs and into their apartment. She was aware of the smell of tobacco and his stubbly cheek. She felt small, very small, enfolded in his strong arms. She began to cry quietly, easily, like a child when all the pain and anger have passed and the tears just come of themselves.

But a smile can break through tears like that, the way the sun breaks through the clouds. The burden is lifted.

You are not alone, she told herself. And when you are not alone, nothing is as hard as it seems at first.

"I want to kiss you," said Lena all of a sudden, and felt her teacher's trembling hands.

"Thank you," whispered her teacher, without having quite understood why Lena had kissed her.

"Let me kiss you, too," said Lena, pressing herself hard to her mother as if to impart some of her own strength to her. Lena's mother kissed her and blinked, though she had not really understood why either.

"And you, too," said Lena, pressing herself to her father, as if drawing on his strength. He held her tightly and whispered, "We'll be moving too." He had understood. Everything.

Lena straightened up and smiled. "Look how I've changed," she said. "Crying and slobbering all over you. But I should be changing—after all, I'm going to be in the ninth grade."

She looked at the three adults, the people closest

to her, and said casually, "Tomorrow is September first. I'll go back to school."

Her mother began blinking, but her father nodded.

"I have to be there," said Lena looking at Vera Ilyinichna. Of the three adults, she was probably the one who knew best what Lena felt she had to do.

18

The first of September was Fedya's first day at his new school. None of his new classmates knew that his father was called John Ivanovich or the American or Uncle Sam. Besides, his father was still acting like a changed man, and so there was no real reason for Fedya to avoid the other boys. Fedya started looking at them with interest, though it was an interest tempered by caution.

After school his mother had put him to work drilling holes in the walls for curtain rods and kitchen shelves. He had expected to finish the job quickly, but soon he saw that he had his hands full—the walls were made of concrete and offered strong resistance to his drill.

And so it was only two days later that he went to see Lena.

First he climbed up the pigeon cote, fed his birds, and let them out to fly. Looking over at Lena's window, he was alarmed to see that the curtains weren't there. He called out to her a few times, but there was no answer.

He climbed back down, ran up the stairs, and rang the doorbell.

He could hear it ringing inside the apartment. He rang again and again, but nobody came to the door. He rang the bell of the next apartment, but nobody answered there either.

He rushed outside and climbed up the drainpipe. When he pressed his face to the window Fedya gasped. It was empty! The walls were bare; the floor, dark in the places where the furniture had been, must have been polished, because it was still gleaming. The last rays of the setting sun caught the tiny carnations on the wallpaper.

Fedya stared at the empty room, as if trying to recall everything down to the last detail, but he couldn't. All he could see was Lena. Lena was all that mattered. There had always been a special aura around her—sometimes joyous, sometimes sad—but it always made everything else seem shadowy and insignificant.

Fedya noticed a little pink rubber doll in a dark

corner by the door. The doll had no clothes on and was lying facedown, its arms flung out to its sides as if it had thrown itself to the floor in despair.

He looked around the empty room one more time, then slid back down the drainpipe. He leaned against the drainpipe and watched his birds.

The sun was setting behind the acacias, but the sky was still clear and translucent—the pigeons swooped and dove as if they were swimming in the blue air.

Something snapped shut inside of Fedya.

He stopped talking to his parents, his mind was a complete blank.

When he was called on in school, he would stand confused, unable to answer questions. The other students started to laugh at him and call him "Dummy." But Fedya never even noticed.

His body seemed to have lost all feeling, and his heart seemed dead. Each day after school he would take the bus to his old neighborhood, feed and fly his pigeons, and then climb the drainpipe that led to Lena's window.

But one day that too came to an end. He found the drainpipe lying on a pile of debris, the wind whistling monotonously through it. And the window, through which Lena had looked out at the world, was also lying on that same pile of debris.

"Hey, kid," called the driver of a steam shovel, loading the debris onto a truck. "You better get your pigeon cote out of there—we're starting on the foundations tomorrow."

Fedya looked numbly at the ruins of their house and remembered the morning when his mother left for work to repay the seven hundred rubles. His parents had been laughing and whispering to each other, but he had woken up with a bad premonition.

So that's how it was. Even the pigeons would have to go. Fedya let them out, but not the way he usually did. This time he picked up each bird individually, stroked its head, and then tossed it up in the air. The pigeons flapped their wings, eager to fly in a flock the way they always did, but he released them one by one, saying good-bye to each one.

The birds soared through the clear autumn sky while Fedya slowly and carefully collected all the remaining wood shavings. The recent sunny weather had dried them, and they rustled crisply as he crumpled them up, giving off a faint woody aroma.

"Got a match?" Fedya asked the steam shovel driver.

"Don't get yourself in trouble," he said with a grin. "Your mother might tan your hide." He tossed Fedya a box of matches, signaling that he could keep them.

When the man had left, Fedya squatted down by the cote. He looked up at the sky again, eagerly, greedily, one last time. The pigeons were circling, separating, then coming back together, a bright cloud of them.

It was beginning to get dark. The pigeons would be coming back to the cote soon.

Fedya climbed back up to the cote. He slammed the cote cover shut and then for some reason put the padlock on it. He took out the matches.

The small flame trembled in his hand, a thin bluish trail of smoke drifting off to one side. Fedya straightened his back and looked out over the old neighborhood. It was all gone now. A few barracks still tottered at the edge of a vast darkness. People had once lived there. There had once been a nice dusty road through there. Now all that was left was the pigeon cote. And two poplars.

Fedya struck another match, touched it to the pile of wood shavings, and climbed down.

A flame shot six feet in the air, the wood began crackling. Fedya looked up and saw his pigeons still flying as if nothing unusual were happening.

He turned and ran.

There were only a few people at the bus stop, but he pushed ahead of the line, blind to everything. A few people cursed him. Fedya stood at the back of the bus looking down at the peaceful gray of the asphalt. But he couldn't stand that for very long and, despite himself, he looked back up at the sky. The pigeons were still circling, suspecting nothing. Fedya rushed to the door and began pounding on it like a madman.

"Driver, stop," someone shouted. "The boy's missed his stop."

The bus came to a halt and the door hissed open. Fedya jumped down, twisting his foot and falling onto one knee. The sharp pain seemed to bring him back to his senses.

His pigeons! How could he abandon them? What right did he have to do that? He remembered that some wise man had said that we are responsible for everything we tame. And he was responsible for those birds.

And he bore a responsibility for Lena too.

He ran back to the flaming pigeon cote. In the

gathering darkness the frenzied birds dashed above the tongues of fire like silent shadows.

Fedya raised his arms and cast a long wavering shadow on the ground. The sight of his shadow gave him strength.

He flung out his arms and the pigeons recognized him. They fluttered over his head and came to rest on his shoulders. They were all cooing in alarm as he gathered them all in and tucked them all inside his jacket, except for two that he kept on his hand. Then he headed for the nearest police station to ask for directions to the boarding school for crippled children. The stern uniformed men listened to Fedya's story with understanding, casting occasional glances at his pigeons.

In the end they drove Fedya to the boarding school in the sidecar of a police motorcycle. Holding his breath, Fedya walked in through the creaking gate and down the long tree-lined path that led to the school.

There were several buildings on the spacious grounds, but there were lights on in only one—a two-story red brick building that looked warm in the last light of day. Noise and gales of laughter were coming from inside. For a moment Fedya felt out of place. His voice soft and uncertain, he shouted.

"Lena! Lena! Lena!"

A shadow fell across a windowpane and the window opened, revealing an old woman's face.

"Who do you want?"

"Lena!"

The woman withdrew, and a moment later, Fedya heard her saying, "There's a boy outside with pigeons."

Lena raced down the corridor in her wheelchair and down the leaf-strewn path, her heart about to leap out of her chest. It was dark now, and she almost collided with Fedya. "You?" she gasped.

He held out a tumbler to her, and she tucked it under her coat, where it began cooing like an infant.

Lena was seized by excitement, alarm, and some other emotion that lifted her, made her sit straight, and filled her lungs with air that was as fresh as spring water.

Fedya stared at her ardently without saying a word while Lena repeated senselessly, "You? You? But why?"

But her words were at odds with her feelings. "Why did you have to find me?" she said, the words pouring out of her now. "There's no sense to it, don't you see that? It'll have to end, sooner or later.

We have to end it ourselves. It'll be easier like that!"

"The pigeon cote's gone," interrupted Fedya. "And your house is gone too."

Lena shivered as she remembered the little enclave and her own house, which had seemed so alien to her, and the cooing of the pigeons and the pungent smell of the wood shavings.

She had known that it had come to an end. Just as seeing Fedya would have to end. But now Fedya was standing before her, holding his pigeons and trembling slightly.

"No, Fedya," she said, not listening to her heart. "It's better that we end it ourselves, here and now."

"I know. But we can't. It's probably how it is when you're grown up. But we aren't grown up yet. And until we are, we shouldn't . . ." He didn't finish his sentence, but Lena understood. And until they were grown up, they shouldn't let themselves be ruled by cold calculations like that. They mustn't!

"We musn't," she said aloud. Fedya nodded.

They didn't hear Nurse Dusya approaching them until she appeared between them, looking first at Fedya, then at Lena. Fedya handed Nurse Dusya a pigeon. Then he got out another, and then another.

"Put them in a cage for now, he said. "I'll be coming back here to make a cote for them.

Nurse Dusya sighed and thrust the pigeons under her robe. The pigeons made a few unhappy sounds but did not resist her. Nurse Dusya turned and shuffled back to the dorm.

They were alone again.

"I'll be coming back to make a cote," said Fedya. "And we, at least until we're grown up . . ."

He bent toward Lena and took her face in his hands.

Lena closed her eyes.

In the dorm someone slammed the window shut.

About the Author

Albert Likhanov was born in Kirov, U.S.S.R. He was a journalism student at the Urals State University in Sverdlovsk and went on to become the Siberian correspondent for a number of newspapers and magazines. Now editor-in-chief of *Smena* magazine, he is the author of twelve works of fiction, all of them dedicated to teenagers.

Format by Constance Fogler
Set in Baskerville
Composed, printed, and bound by The Haddon Craftsmen
HARPER & ROW, PUBLISHERS, INC.